MATT

Texas Rascals Book Two

LORI WILDE

Created with Vellum

I

"I hate to trouble you, Miss Savannah, but I'm afraid I've got more bad news." Clement Olson stood in the doorway staring down at his dusty cowboy boots and clutching a battered, paint-stained baseball cap between gnarled, callused fingers.

"Clem, I don't think I can handle another disaster right now," Savannah Markum mumbled around a mouthful of straight pins and glanced up from where she knelt on the kitchen floor pinning the hem on her younger sister's wedding dress.

Ginger stood before her on a chair, arms outstretched, billows of white lace and satin draped over her petite frame. Savannah's fifteen-month-old son, Cody, toddled across the room, his chubby fingers wrapped around a plastic, drool-soaked teething ring.

Savannah plucked the pins from her mouth and stabbed them into a tomato-shaped pincushion. "Let me guess, the work truck finally called it quits."

"No, ma'am." Clem shifted his weight, and then met her gaze. "I'm afraid it's more serious than that."

What now? Between her overdue property taxes, an astronomical vet bill, and a busted washing machine, finances loomed as bleak as the west Texas landscape.

Not to mention Ginger's wedding expenses.

A heavy strand of honey-colored hair broke free from her ponytail and flopped across her forehead. Irritated, Savannah brushed away the uncooperative lock and rose to her feet.

"Clem?" she asked. His grim manner alarmed her. "What's happened?"

"Fourteen of the Gerts are missing."

"What?" The herd of purebred Santa Gertrudis cattle had been Gary's pride and joy. She furrowed her brow. "Are you sure?"

Clem winced and nodded. "I figure somebody stole 'em in the wee hours of the morning, Miss Savannah. I'm sorry I didn't discover it sooner."

Savannah blew out her breath through puffed cheeks. No point in panicking...*yet.* "Maybe there's a break in the fence line, and they've wandered out onto the road."

Clem shook his gray head. "'Fraid not. Julio and I scouted the whole spread for two hours. Didn't find a single downed fence, but we did find something I think you should see."

Savannah whispered a curse. When she'd promised her late husband that she would continue running the ranch as an investment in Cody's future, she hadn't realized just how much responsibility she'd be assuming.

Family, friends, neighbors, nearly everyone she knew advised her to sell out. But she'd signed a prenup that prevented her from selling the ranch. She didn't tell people about the prenup because it was none of their business. In a town like Rascal, everyone felt like they had a right to snoop in your personal affairs.

Her relationship with her late husband was complicated. Although she had cared for Gary—he'd been a kind man—

their marriage had been one of convenience. Gary gave her stability and a soft place to land after the chaos of her mother's death to breast cancer. And she'd given the Markum ranch a legacy it would otherwise not have had.

Cody.

Savannah felt the old guilt swell inside her. She wouldn't break her vow to forever keep their secret. She owed Gary that much.

"Let's go." Savannah headed for the door.

Cody let out a squeal of delight. She turned to see her son gleefully digging in a pot of ivy and shoveling a fistful of dirt into his mouth.

"Could you catch him, Ginger?"

"Can't. I'm still pinned into my wedding dress." Ginger lifted her shoulders in a helpless shrug.

Savannah sighed. She needed twenty hands and two heads. In two long-legged strides, she crossed the floor and reached down to pull her son onto her hip.

"Shew." She gently brushed the dirt from his tongue with her fingers. "Nasty."

Cody grinned. The baby looked so much like his father it hurt.

Conflicting emotions knotted Savannah's chest. The pain was as sharp now as it had been two years ago when she'd learned she was pregnant, just as her mother lay dying.

"We'll be right back," she told Ginger, then followed Clem outside, Cody still clinging to her neck. She savored the solid feel of her son pressed to her side and smelled his sweet baby scent.

The elderly ranch hand led her to the battered old work truck and opened the door for Savannah to climb inside. He pumped the starter, coaxed the ailing engine to life, drove a quarter mile down the bumpy, rutted road and braked at the west pasture gate.

They got out and walked through the high Johnson grass slapping at their shins.

"Padlock's been cut." Clem pointed out the severed lock dangling from the rusty hasp.

"Don't touch it," Savannah said. "Evidence for the sheriff."

Clem grunted, tugging the baseball cap's bill down on his forehead. "There's more. See those tire tracks?"

Savannah studied the fresh tracks rutted into the moist earth where it had rained several days earlier. "Yes."

"Trailer tracks. Don't belong to none of our vehicles. Weren't out here yesterday."

"How did the thieves get this far back on the ranch without you or Julio hearing them?" Savannah asked.

Cody squirmed in her arms, and she shifted him to the other hip.

Clem shrugged, looked sheepish. "We both had a little too much to drink last night. Slept pretty soundly."

Savannah caught her bottom lip between her teeth, gazed at the ten Santa Gertrudis left grazing in the field. Who had stolen her cattle? She hated to think it was someone from Rascal.

She thought briefly about calling her nearest neighbor, former Chicago cop, Keegan Winslow. Keegan had recently married her best friend, Wren. Wren taught English at Rascal High, and Keegan now ran her small dairy. He would be happy to look around and give her his opinion, but she needed proper help.

"What are you gonna do?" Clem asked.

"The only thing I can do," Savannah said. "Call the sheriff."

DETECTIVE MATTHEW FORRESTER GUIDED HIS BRAND-spanking-new, government-issue four-wheel-drive Jeep Cherokee down the gravel country road. His heart raced like a Palomino on steroids.

What in the Sam Hill was wrong with him? He was going to the Circle B to investigate the report of stolen cattle. The fact that Savannah Markum owned the ranch would not affect his objectivity in any way.

Liar.

Who was he kidding?

The idea of seeing her again had him sweating.

Despite what he'd told himself during the past two years, he hadn't gotten over her—not for a day, not for an hour, not for one minute. Savannah Raylene Prentiss Markum had broken his heart.

But he would never, ever let her know that. He refused to give her that much power over him again.

He turned into the Circle B's driveway and killed the engine. For a moment, he sat there, hands on the wheel, the air inside the Jeep growing heated, heavy. Simply taking a breath required his complete concentration.

Be cool as granite. You're a professional. Not some head-over-heels kid.

Grabbing his notebook, Matt unlatched his seatbelt and slid out of the vehicle. "Geronimo," he mumbled and started up the front steps.

At the door, he paused, fist poised to knock, when he saw the baby.

The toddler stood knee-high, his face pressed against the screen door. He looked up at Matt and grinned a big, toothless grin.

Jolting pain stronger than any electrical current lambasted Matt's heart. Savannah's kid. Gary Markum's kid.

The baby that should have been *his*.

Staggered, Matt took a step backward. He knew that

she'd had a baby, but he hadn't expected to react like this. The local gossips had made it their duty to keep him abreast of Savannah's doings. He'd been informed when her mother had lost her battle with breast cancer and when Markum had also died of cancer a little over a year ago.

But even to himself, Matt refused to admit that Savannah's widow status had persuaded him to come back to Rascal. He'd returned because Patrick Langley had offered him a job as a detective for Presidio County and for no other reason.

Well, that and Rascal was home.

The baby wriggled with excitement, then promptly fell onto his diapered bottom.

"Cody?" Savannah's voice wafted through the screen door, freezing Matt to the front porch. He wasn't ready for this—seeing her up close and personal for the first time in two years.

"What are you doing, Cody Coo?" She stepped to the foyer, bent down to retrieve her child, and stopped in midmotion. Straightening, she turned her head.

Time hung suspended.

The past and future did not exist.

Only the present moment was real as their eyes met through the screen door.

Savannah was even more beautiful than he remembered. Her hair, the color of light brown sugar frosted with streaks of honey, feathered back from her oval face in attractive layers. Her hazel eyes, a tantalizing shade of golden green, rounded in surprise.

She wore cutoff blue jeans, a white sleeveless blouse, and flip-flops. Her once skinny figure had blossomed with childbearing, spreading out into delightful curves. Her wonderful vanilla scent floated through the mesh wire of the screen door and enveloped him in a glove of warm, soft memories.

She smelled just the same. Like Christmas cookies and homemade ice cream.

"What are you doing here?" she asked at last. The sound of her rich, coffee-and-cream voice rocked his very soul. She seemed so cool, so calm, so detached.

It hurt, that easy detachment.

His throat narrowed, and he feared he couldn't speak. Matt fixed his gaze on her long, slender arms.

Scooping up the baby, she cradled him to her side as if using her child as a buffer between them.

"Sheriff Langley sent me," he explained. "I'm the new investigator for Presidio County."

Savannah hesitated only a second before reaching over and unlatching the screen door. "Won't you come in?"

Goodness gracious. Savannah struggled valiantly to keep her face from reflecting her feelings. She had no idea Matt Forrester was back in town and working for the sheriff's department.

She felt dizzy, breathless. The man still held the astounding ability to affect her unlike anyone else on earth.

He crossed the threshold just inches from her.

Savannah stepped back and cradled her free arm against her body because she longed to reach out and touch him, to run her fingers over his tanned skin, to convince herself that he was real. But she'd willingly relinquished any proprietary hold on him long ago.

They stood in silence, each of them warily assessing the other.

Matt's shoulders had broadened. His jaw had hardened, too, giving him an authoritative air. Tiny lines etched his forehead, and his eyes held a suspicious glint. He'd definitely changed, grown tougher, more rugged. He had a different aura about him—calculated, controlled, contained—less like TNT, more like cyanide.

The thought jarred her.

He wore snakeskin cowboy boots, a casual-cut gray sports jacket over an aqua Western-style shirt. Matt had always looked good in that color. It complemented his jet-black hair and straight, white teeth.

She caught herself studying his mouth and quickly jerked her gaze away. Helplessly, she remembered his passionate, yet gentle kisses, the gruff sounds of his throaty laughter, the security of his sheltering arms.

But this Matt differed from the man of her memory. She sensed kissing this Matt would not be the same. Time and circumstance had altered them both.

"Tell me about your missing cattle," he said in a businesslike fashion as if they shared no collective memories.

Does he have any lingering feelings for me at all? Savannah immediately squelched the thought. It didn't matter. Yesterday was gone forever.

"We believe they were stolen."

Cody reached for a strand of her hair and stuck it into his mouth. She disentangled herself from her baby's soggy grasp.

"Is this your son?" His tone was even.

Fear fluttered in her heart. "Yes. His name is Cody."

Cody was Matt's middle name. Did a fleeting glimpse of agony flash through Matt's eyes, or was it her imagination? If only she hadn't—well, she *had*, hadn't she—no point rehashing a past she could not change.

Matt cleared his throat. "Handsome boy. He takes after you."

She ducked her head, embarrassed. "Thanks."

Ginger trotted into the living room, swatches of fabric in her hand. "'Vannah, should I go with the rose or mauve for the tablecloths?" She stopped dead in her tracks. "Oh," she exclaimed, looking from Savannah to Matt and back again. "Oh."

"Hello, Ginger. Nice to see you," Matt greeted her politely.

Ginger lifted her eyebrows in surprise. "Um...hi."

"Matt's here to investigate the stolen cattle," Savannah explained. "He's working for the sheriff's department now."

"Well, I hope you catch whoever did it," Ginger blurted. "Losing those Santa Gertrudis could send Savannah into bankruptcy."

She shot her sister a dirty look. Too often Ginger spoke before she thought. The last thing Savannah wanted was for Matt Forrester to know about her dire financial straits. She couldn't bear his pity.

Matt pursed his lips but said nothing.

"Here, watch Cody." Savannah handed the baby to her sister.

Ginger dropped her swatches on the coffee table and accepted her nephew.

"Come on." Savannah waved at Matt. "Let me show you the west pasture."

❧

MATT FOLLOWED HER THROUGH THE FARMHOUSE AND OUT the back door. His eyes locked on her swaying backside. Sharp shards of pure sexual need jabbed his gut. Would he ever stop desiring this woman? And why did he still want her after the hell she'd put him through?

She stopped and turned to face him. Afternoon sunlight filtered through the mesquite trees, highlighting her classic features in a rosy glow. He tried desperately to ignore the arousal growing inside him.

"Let's take my Jeep," he said.

They got inside, and Matt maneuvered the vehicle across the pasture. He noticed she gripped the hand strap with her right arm, her muscles tense.

"Just follow the path," she directed. "Turn right at the fork."

From the corner of his eye, he saw Savannah lean forward, holding herself stiffly as if relaxing against the seat might make her more vulnerable somehow.

She stared straight ahead.

He remembered a time when she would have been plastered against his side, her arm tucked through his as they drove, her head nestled on his shoulder while her sly little tongue snaked out to burn hot licks and kisses along his neck.

Matt shivered at the thought.

Other memories rushed through his mind—the possessive thirst they'd had for each other, the desperate need to be together, all ruined by Savannah's fickleness. He'd been unable to assuage her fears. Unable to prove his loyalty to her no matter how hard he'd tried. She'd been so sure that he would leave her, that she'd shut the door on their love before it ever really had a chance to flourish.

And then that fateful night, when he finally gathered the courage to tell her that he loved her, and she hadn't said it back. Had in fact broken up with him. Telling him that his dangerous job was a deal breaker.

Matt winced. Unrequited love was the pits.

Lord knows he'd tried to talk to her, to ask if they could at least remain friends while he held on to the hope that she could come to love him the way he loved her. But she'd told him a clean break was best. Then she'd stopped taking his calls and returning his texts.

After a while, he stopped trying. She'd been clear enough. And a man had his pride.

If she didn't want him, she didn't want him.

That's all there was to it.

The next thing he knew, she'd married Gary Markum, and that had killed the last of his hopes.

The old pain crested in his heart—sharp, raw, as fresh as yesterday. God, he thought he'd put all that behind him. Thought he could handle coming home to Rascal. Thought he could handle seeing her again.

He'd miscalculated her power over him.

Even now, two years later.

Matt gripped the steering wheel and peered through the windshield at the narrow pasture road. He shouldn't keep torturing himself like this. The past was over. His purpose for being here had nothing to do with Savannah and everything to do with the recent rash of cattle thefts in Presidio County.

Concentrate, Forrester, he chided himself. You've got a job to tend.

He could ignore Savannah's cool vanilla scent and those firm, tanned legs stretched long across the floorboard. He could overlook the husky tones of her deep velvet voice. Deny the smoky fires she kindled inside him.

Or, if he had to think about her, he would remember the misery she'd caused him.

They jostled over a bump in the road, and Matt felt the Jeep's throbbing vibration clean through the seat.

"Stop here," she said.

Relieved, Matt trod on the brakes. He wasted no time bailing out of the vehicle then shook his head to dispel his disturbing thoughts. He walked to the gate. Instinct and training kicked in. Matt squatted and scanned the site.

A damaged lock. Rutted tire marks. Heavy vehicle, trailer probably. A jumble of cattle hoofprints.

Something red caught his eye. A plastic cocktail straw chewed up on the end. He sighed and ran a hand across his stubbled jaw. Bagged and tagged the straw, in case it meant anything, and the severed padlock.

"I need a detailed description of the cattle," he said after he'd stowed the padlock and straw into evidence bags.

Savannah crossed her arms over her chest, tipped her head back, and looked down her nose at him as she described the cattle.

"Were they branded?"

"Of course." She pointed at the ten remaining Gerts clustered along the fence row. "A circle with a backward B."

"How much were they worth?"

"Four grand apiece. Seven for the bull."

Matt nodded. "That's felony larceny, and since they cut the padlock and came at night, we might be able to add a burglary charge. Carries a stiffer sentence." He got to his feet and dusted his fingertips together. "I want to interview your ranch hands. Who are they?"

"I've only got two left—Clem Olson and Julio Diaz."

"I don't know this Julio fellow. Is he new in town?"

"Hired him about three months ago."

"What kind of references does he have?"

She lifted her shoulders in a defensive gesture. "Julio showed up willing to work for what I could pay."

Matt stared at her, incredulous. "You didn't check his references?"

"Unfortunately, I don't have the luxury of being choosy. He's the only one who applied for the job."

"How do you know he's not an illegal?" Matt chided, disturbed by her glib trust in a total stranger.

"I don't."

"You'd be breaking the law, Savannah."

"He showed me a social security card."

"Those can be faked."

She wrinkled her nose at him. "Are you going to arrest me, Matt?"

Damn that hardheaded streak of hers. Frustrated, he plowed a hand through his hair. "You allow a total stranger to stay at your ranch without checking his background? Two women and a baby living all alone out here."

She shrugged.

"Very foolhardy, Mrs. Markum." He forced himself to say her married name. The word "Markum" caught in his throat, bitter as gall.

"Clem lives here, too."

"Yeah. But Clem as old as the hills and twice as slow."

"That's why I had to hire a younger man to do the ranch work." Her tone held a bit of acid.

"You still should have checked him out."

"I trust Julio. He's very loyal."

Unlike you. Immediately, Matt was ashamed of his unkind thought. It wasn't like him. But damn if that old hurt hadn't crawled up to the surface of his skin.

"Are you finished raking me over the coals?"

Her blind trust in this Julio character made him want to suck ground glass. Didn't she realize she'd laid herself wide open for trouble? Whatever had happened to those Santa Gertrudis, Julio Diaz could be involved. Matt met her bold gaze, narrowed his eyes, and mentally dared her to look away.

She stared him down, rising to his unspoken challenge. "Well?"

2

Looking deep into those murky brown eyes, Savannah inhaled fiercely. She felt as if she'd hit a brick wall traveling ninety miles an hour—shattered, splattered, gone.

"Do you think I might speak to the trustworthy Mr. Diaz?" Matt's tone oozed sarcasm.

"He's gone into town."

"Convenient."

"What are you suggesting?"

"Nothing. Merely making an observation."

"Maybe you should keep your observations to yourself." Why was she being prickly?

"May be."

They stood like two warriors. Each ready for battle, but neither quite sure why they were fighting.

Savannah finally dropped her gaze, unable to continue the intensity. Looking at him brought back all the old pain, the loneliness, the moments of despair, precipitated by that awful night at Kelly's bar after he'd been shot trying to break up a fight.

Briefly, she closed her eyes and swallowed hard, remembering the scene as if it were yesterday—the dark interior of Kelly's noisy, smoky bar. Crowded on a Saturday evening in Rascal, Texas with cowpokes and their girls. The jukebox blaring Hank Williams's "I'm So Lonesome I Could Cry" just before the fight broke out.

"How about Clem?" he asked.

"Huh?" Savannah blinked herself back to the present.

"Is he here? I'd like to question him about the disappearing cattle."

"Yeah. Sure. Clem is in the barn."

"Anything else missing?" Matt arched an eyebrow.

"I don't know."

"Better check on that, too. The thieves have been taking ranching equipment along with the cattle. Even stole one of your neighbor's gold-plated rodeo belt buckle."

"Who?"

"Kurt McNally."

"So there have been other robberies?"

Matt nodded.

"You think it's an organized ring?"

"Yes, I do. I'll need for you to inventory your supplies."

"Okay."

"Let's go talk to Clem."

The awkward silence grew as they drove to her farmhouse. So much lay between them, unresolved, unspoken, buried beneath the surface ready to explode. Matt held his shoulders rigid, his jaw clenched tight.

"So, you've got yourself a ranch," he said at last.

Savannah wasn't sure how to respond. "Gary left the ranch to me, yes."

"Is that why you married him, Savannah? To get your hands on the Circle B?"

She stared at him. Was that what Matt really thought of

her? Did he believe her to be so mercenary that she'd marry for money?

If he only knew the truth!

And as far as money went, well, she hovered one step away from bankruptcy. Gary's medical bills had eaten up a large chunk of his money, leaving little to run the ranch. The loss of the Gerts made things worse since she'd intended on selling some of them to pay for Ginger's wedding.

"I married Gary because he was a good, honest man." Who promised to be a loving father to her son as long as she never let anyone know that Cody wasn't his.

"But did you love him?" The word "*love*" broke brittle against Matt's tongue, like the sound of cracking glass.

"I don't think that's any of your business."

Matt snorted. "I never really knew you, did I, Savannah?"

What could she possibly say to that? "I suppose not."

At one time, she'd thought she knew everything about Matt Forrester—his affinity for Dutch chocolate ice cream on a waffle cone, his dislike of social media, the salty taste of his skin, his hopes and dreams of one day becoming sheriff of Presidio County.

The same dreams that had driven the initial wedge between them. Matt's law enforcement ambitions had always troubled her, and after he'd been wounded, it had been too much for her to take. Now, she realized just how foolishly naive she'd really been. She'd never known what was in his heart.

He stopped the Jeep outside the barn. Relieved, Savannah got out, anxious to distance herself from this man who dredged up a past she wanted desperately to forget.

"Clem," she called out, aware of Matt following doggedly in her tracks.

The elderly ranch hand appeared in the doorway of the

barn, wiping his hands on an oil-smeared rag. “Whatcha need, Miss Savannah?”

“Mr. Forrester would like to speak with you about the missing cattle.”

“Oh.” Clem shifted his weight and dropped his gaze.

Matt pulled a black notebook and a pen from his pocket. He moved forward and extended his hand. “Hello, Clem, do you remember me?”

Clem nodded and grasped Matt’s hand but quickly let go. “Sure do, you’re Asa Forrester’s boy.”

“That’s right.”

Clem sized Matt up with a sideways glance. “Done pretty good for yourself, I see.”

“I was lucky enough to get the job I wanted.”

Lucky, hell. Savannah knew Matt had poured his heart and soul into pursuing a law enforcement career. Hard work, determination, and personal sacrifice had landed him the job. She was proud of him, even if she did hate the danger that came with the job.

“Yeah,” Clem said. “Some of us ain’t been so lucky.”

“I want you to tell me about the missing cattle.” Matt waited, pen poised over the notepad.

“Mind if I smoke?” Clem asked, digging in his shirt pocket with nicotine-stained fingers for a pack of cigarettes.

“You nervous, Clem?” Matt asked.

“Me? Nah. Why should I be nervous?” Clem struck a match, fumbling it to the ground.

Savannah noticed his hand trembled slightly as he tried again, this time succeeding in his attempt to light the cigarette.

Matt pursed his lips. “I don’t know, Clem, you tell me.”

“I ain’t got nothin’ to hide.”

“That’s good.” Matt gave the man a dangerous smile. “Then you haven’t got anything to worry about.”

"Are you accusing me of somethin'?" Clem took a drag off his cigarette.

"Just doing my job, Mr. Olson."

Clem sent Savannah a beseeching glance. "You don't think I stole them cows, do you, Miss Savannah?"

"Of course not, Clem." She glared at Matt. Why was he badgering the elderly man? Clem was obviously too old to be a threat. Besides, he'd worked for Gary's family for over twenty years. If Matt thought Clem was involved, he was barking up the wrong tree.

"It's my duty to be suspicious of everyone." Matt sent Savannah a look so cool that it startled her. Did he consider her a suspect, too? What rubbish. Why would she steal her own cattle?

"We first noticed something unusual when Julio and I went out to feed this morning." The cigarette seemed to have boosted Clem's confidence.

"What did you see?" Matt quizzed.

Clem shrugged. "West pasture gate hanging open. We drove closer and saw the busted lock."

"Is that when you reported the thefts to Mrs. Markum?"

"No."

"When did you report it?"

"Lunchtime."

"Why did you wait?"

An uneasy expression crossed Clem's face. "Didn't want to worry her needlessly. She's got enough troubles right now. I wanted to make sure the Gerts hadn't just gotten out before I alarmed her."

"How very gallant of you," Matt mocked.

When had he become so hard? The Matt she remembered was kindhearted and generous to a fault. Had working in law enforcement changed him, or was it something else?

"Julio and I searched for a downed fence," Clem continued. "We kept hoping the cattle had just wandered off."

"Rather optimistic. So how long after you discovered the cattle missing did you report this to Mrs. Markum?"

"About five hours."

"Five hours?"

"Yes."

"Long time to wait, isn't it?"

"I dunno."

"Why did you wait five hours, Clem? Don't you realize it's important to report a crime as soon as possible? For all your stalling, the cattle could be in Mexico by now." Matt's face darkened.

"I... I...just wanted to protect Miss Savannah," Clem stuttered.

"Leave him alone," Savannah said.

Matt turned on his heels to face her. "You got a problem?"

"This isn't a trial, and you're not a prosecutor. Stop harassing him."

"Do you want me to take him in for questioning?"

"No, sir," Clem said. "I'll cooperate."

"Thank you," Matt told the older man. "Now, did you or Julio see or hear anything out of the ordinary over the last few days? Any strangers hanging around? People asking questions about the ranch? Anything like that?"

Clem shook his head.

"What do you think about Julio Diaz?"

"He's a hard worker."

"Does he ever have visitors?"

"Nope. Real quiet. Keeps to himself." Clem relaxed a little, crushing the spent cigarette butt beneath the toe of his boot.

"Have you noticed anything else missing?" Matt asked.

Clem shook his head.

"Think real hard." Matt stepped forward, thrusting out his chest in an intimidating stance. "Any equipment missing? Saddles? Barrels? Feed? Rope? Even something as simple as gardening tools?"

"No, sir."

Savannah folded her arms. She'd never seen this authoritative side of Matt—the inquisitive, hard-nosed detective. And although she dreaded having him so close, she was glad he was on the case. If anyone could get her cattle returned, Matt could.

He looked at Savannah. "You, too. I want an inventory of your equipment. I want to know if even one nail is missing."

"Why are you so sure they took more than just the cattle?" Savannah asked.

"Because in the last three months, there have been six thefts in this county, and each and every time, as I said before, the robbers took supplies as well as cattle. Usually, things they could pawn quickly. Now, please get that inventory list together for me."

Savannah raised her chin. As if she had time for that. "After I finish sewing the zipper into Ginger's wedding dress."

"No," Matt corrected. "You'll make it your first priority."

Anger flared inside her. Who did he think he was? Thank heavens she hadn't been stupid enough to marry such a bossy, opinionated male. "Listen here, Matt Forrester."

"Could I have a glass of water?" He interrupted her.

"Of course." Savannah led him across the yard, through the back door, and into the kitchen. Cody sat in his high chair, happily spitting mashed potatoes at Ginger. Savannah got Matt a glass of water just as the phone at his waistband rang. He set down the glass and picked up his phone.

"What's up?" her younger sister mouthed silently.

Savannah shrugged, took the bowl of potatoes from

Ginger, and smiled at her son. "Come on, Cody Coo, eat a bite for Mama."

Cody waved his hands and shook his head.

Savannah pretended to be engrossed in feeding her son, but she couldn't help listening to Matt's conversation.

"Forrester here," Matt growled into the phone. He turned his back on Savannah and Ginger. Lowered his voice. "What's up?"

"Isn't this awful?" Ginger whispered in Savannah's ear. "Matt Forrester, of all people, assigned to our case."

Savannah rolled her eyes, but her heart gave a little hop. It wasn't awful. Not at all.

"When?" Matt asked the person on the other end of the line. "Right. I'll get on it immediately. Thanks for the tip, Megan. I owe you."

Megan? Who was she?

Matt hung up the phone, then turned to face Savannah. "I've got to go," he said.

"Something more important?"

Matt pulled a key fob from his pocket and shot her a sidelong glance. "Remember I told you about Kurt McNally's gold belt buckle?"

"Uh-huh."

"Some pawn owner reported a guy trying to hock Kurt's belt buckle in San Antonio."

"You're going to San Antonio?"

"Yep."

"Now?"

"It's my job. Good thing you married a rancher instead of a sheriff's detective, eh, Savvy."

Savvy.

The old term of endearment sliced through her, barbed-wire sharp. No one but Matt had ever called her Savvy.

"What am I supposed to do in the meantime?" she asked, following him to the front door.

"Keep your eyes and ears open, make out that inventory list. I'll be back as soon as I can to speak to Mr. Diaz."

She raised a hand to her throat. For the first time, a tug of fear ate at her. She, Ginger, and the baby were alone, isolated, unprotected.

"What if the thieves come back?"

An arrogant grin crossed his face. "Why, darlin', you just tell them Detective Matt Forrester is on their case."

And with that, he leaned down and planted a quick kiss on her startled lips...then he turned and swaggered out the door.

3

Why in Sam Hill had he kissed her?

What had he been thinking? Had he lost his ever loving mind?

Still, the look on Savannah's face had been priceless. Matt had definitely caught her off guard, but that brief brushing of their lips had undone him, too. There was no denying it, the sparks remained, just as hot and electric as ever.

Matt guided the Jeep onto the freeway, heading east to San Antonio. His behavior had been unprofessional. He couldn't allow himself to be sidetracked by Savannah. He had to stop thinking of her. Had to quit visualizing her long legs, her soft flesh pressed flush against his skin, her fingers entwined in his hair.

Her.

"Ugh!" He groaned aloud and shook his head. This had to stop.

He switched on the satellite radio to an all-news station in an attempt to empty his head. *Concentrate on the thefts. Piece together the puzzle. Review the evidence. Anything.* Anything at all to eliminate the intoxicating vision of Savannah Markum from his brain.

Fact—in the course of the last three months, six ranches had been robbed and over fifty head of cattle stolen in Presidio County. Various ranching and farming equipment had also been taken, including saddles, bridles, baling wire, lanterns, Kurt McNally's gold belt buckle, posthole diggers, even a tractor.

Most of the burglaries occurred at night or when the owners were out of town. The perpetrator had to be someone familiar with the area and the comings and goings of the local residents. Matt knew that much for sure.

But he had few clues. Until Kurt's belt buckle. The thieves were making him feel like a fool, and Matt Forrester hated to be one-upped. He would not be defeated.

For the last two years, since Savannah broke up with him after he got shot and told her that he loved her, he'd funneled all his energy into law enforcement. He lived it, breathed it, reveled in it. The job sustained him, nourished him, fed him through that dark period in his life after Savannah married another man.

The experience honed him into a razor-sharp detective. He should *thank* Savannah for dumping him.

And yet, things could have been so different. He winced. Savannah should have been his wife, Cody, his child.

She'd even named the boy after him. Why? What did that mean?

"It means nothing, Forrester," he growled. "Nada, zip, zero."

Savannah had made her choice, and no amount of wishing could change that fact. Yet, here he was thinking about her again.

Resolutely, Matt pushed thoughts of her aside. Tonight, he had a mission in San Antonio. Tonight, he would focus on his job. Tonight, he would erase Savannah from his brain, for tomorrow would be soon enough to face her and the tangled shreds of their complicated past.

HUMIDITY HUNG HEAVY IN THE BARN'S DANK INTERIOR. Savannah wiped a fine film of perspiration from her brow. Cody lay sleeping in the papoose on her back.

Even with Clem and Ginger's help, taking inventory of the supplies ate up most of the morning. After breakfast, Savannah sent Julio to move the remaining Santa Gertrudis herd from the back pasture to the front acreage next to the house. Savannah wasn't taking any more chances. She wanted the cattle close so she could personally keep an eye on them.

"How much longer?" Ginger complained, wrinkling her nose. "It stinks in here."

"Whining doesn't help matters," Savannah said matter-of-factly.

At twenty-one, and four years Savannah's junior, Ginger sometimes acted much younger. Savannah supposed it was her own fault. She'd spoiled her sister after Mom's death. She'd tried to give her all the advantages she'd never had. Like college and an expensive, formal wedding. And yes, marrying Gary had figured into it.

"Well, I'm glad Todd isn't a rancher," Ginger replied. "I can't wait to move to San Antonio. I always said I'd marry a man who made a living with his brain and not his brawn."

"Todd is a hard worker," Savannah agreed. Her future brother-in-law had already made a reputation for himself in insurance sales, and he was only twenty-five.

"He says I don't even have to work after we get married if I don't want to." Her sister was employed as the office manager at the same insurance firm as Todd. "I can't wait to start having babies." Ginger patted her flat tummy.

"Cody and I are going to miss you, sis."

"Oh, Vannah, it's not you I want to leave." Ginger hugged Savannah as best she could with Cody on her back. "I'm going to miss you, too."

"You'll be too busy getting settled to even think about me. Besides, San Antonio's not at the end of the earth."

"You're the greatest sister anyone could hope for."

"I love you." A tear collected at the corner of Savannah's eye. It was difficult to accept Ginger as grown and married. The rambling farmhouse would be lonelier with her gone.

"Miss Savannah, as far as I can tell, nothing's missing," Clem interrupted. He climbed down off the stepladder and dusted his hands on the seat of his overalls.

Matt would be disappointed. He'd been so sure the thieves had taken equipment along with the Gerts. At the thought of him, she frowned and checked the time on her cell phone.

It was almost noon.

She'd expected him before now. Maybe he'd found her cattle in San Antonio. That would be a relief. She wanted this thing wrapped up, her livestock returned, and Matt eliminated from her life for good, before she did something she'd promised Gary she would never do and spill the beans.

"What about the shotgun Gary used to keep in here for rattlesnakes? Is it missing?" she asked Clem.

"Nope. It's mounted on the wall behind the door." Clem nodded.

"I'm going to start lunch," Ginger said. "You want me to take Cody?"

"Please." Savannah untied the papoose straps from around her middle. "He's getting too heavy for this. My back is killing me."

Cody whimpered awake during the transfer, and Ginger carried him into the house.

Savannah groaned and stretched. The sound of a vehicle turning into the driveway drew her attention. She stepped through the open barn door and caught sight of the cherry red Jeep.

Speak of the devil.

Matt unfurled his long body from the front seat of the vehicle and stalked across the yard toward her. His silhouette ignited a flame of sultry weight in the pit of her stomach. She yearned to launch herself into his embrace, feel his grip tighten around her in that way of his that had once made her feel so safe. She wanted to pull him down in a haystack and kiss him long, slow, and sweet just as they had that very first time they'd kissed on his uncle's farm so long ago.

She still remembered the stars twinkling above, the straw caught in his hair, his hardy, masculine smell tantalizing her nose—a hearty combination of leather, earth, and sunshine. Even now, a shaft of desire cut through her so intense that it took her breath away.

"Dang," Savannah mumbled as their gazes met and held.

He was one fine hunk of man. Tall, well-built, rugged. A man she could count on to save her life in a pinch. A breeze lifted a lock of his coal-black hair, giving him a rakish look.

Her heart thudded faster.

He stepped closer.

That damned kiss he'd given her yesterday had kept her awake half the night.

His eyes hardened, and his mouth turned grim. He assessed her, raking his gaze up and down her body.

She raised a hand to her throat, suddenly aware of her disheveled appearance. Her hair drooped limply from its ponytail. The threads from her cutoff jeans hung like tattered flags down her legs. Her T-shirt was stained with grease and barn grime. Taking a deep breath, she clasped her elbows in her palms and waited for him to speak.

"Afternoon, Savannah." He nodded curtly.

"Matt."

He shifted, settled back into the heels of his boots, and rested his hands on his belt buckle. He said nothing else.

"How was San Antonio?"

"Informative."

"You didn't happen to find my cattle, did you?" The air between them fairly shimmered with tension, like a rubber band stretched to the snapping point. She cringed inwardly, waiting for it to snap.

"No. Did you inventory your supplies?"

"Nothing was missing, least not as far as I can tell. But Gary might have bought some items neither Clem nor I knew anything about."

"Did Gary keep good records on his ranching transactions?"

"Of course."

"Could you make those records available to me?"

She narrowed her eyes. "Why?"

"Routine procedure."

"I don't understand what Gary's papers have to do with my cattle being stolen."

"I need them to verify ownership and the value of the cattle."

"What do you think you'll find?"

"Won't know till I find it."

His evasiveness bothered her. She had a bad feeling about this. What was he hiding? "I see no reason to give you Gary's personal records."

"You don't have a choice, Savannah. This is a criminal investigation, and his paperwork is evidence. Turn them over to me...*now*. Unless you have something to hide."

❧

Did she have something to hide?

Matt pursed his lips. He couldn't tell her that he suspected the theft of her cattle had nothing to do with the other five thefts. That hers was a copycat crime.

The trip to San Antonio had paid off. He'd found the man who'd tried to hock Kurt McNally's belt buckle at a pawn shop sleeping off a bender in the local drunk tank. For the favor of being bailed out of jail, the man had been very willing to talk. The fellow said he'd purchased the buckle off three men in San Antonio. He claimed they'd boasted about stealing cattle and equipment, yet their modus operandi did not match the robbery at the Circle B.

A clearer picture emerged.

The thieves generally grabbed just a few head of cattle grazing in a pasture by the roadside and took all the equipment that wasn't locked up. So why hadn't they stolen any of Savannah's supplies?

He needed Gary Markum's records to ascertain the herd's number, purchase orders, veterinary records, branding accounts, anything that might be helpful in tracking the thieves.

The back door creaked open.

They both turned.

Ginger stepped out onto the porch, shading her eyes against the sun. "Are you staying for lunch, Matt?"

He was about to refuse when he saw Savannah shake her head and lance her sister a dirty look. He grinned. Evidently, Mrs. Markum didn't relish his company.

"We're having fried chicken," Ginger tempted.

"That's my favorite. I'd love to stay, Ginger; thank you for the invitation." He looked at Savannah.

Her frown deepened. “Great,” she muttered and went into the house ahead of him.

Matt chuckled. He liked being a burr under her saddle. Paybacks were hell.

The delicious aroma of frying chicken filled the large farmhouse kitchen.

Ginger stood at the stove, an apron tied around her waist, a pair of tongs in one hand. Cody sat in the middle of the floor, banging on an overturned pan with a wooden spoon. The sight of the little shaver twisted a knife of longing deep in Matt’s chest.

He’d lost so much to stubbornness and false pride. He and Savannah had once shared a bushel of dreams, dreams now scattered, blown to the wind like dandelion seeds.

Why was he torturing himself like this? Wishing, hoping, yearning for a past that could never be recaptured.

“Would you like to wash up?” Savannah asked.

“Where’s the bathroom?” Matt asked.

“This way.” She inclined her head, her shoulders held stiff.

He followed her down the corridor. His eyes devouring the sight of her rounded bottom encased so enticingly in those ragged cutoff jeans, the firm muscles in her long, slender legs flexing as she walked.

The shock of desire racing through his body stunned him like the charge from a cattle prod. After all this time, his desire for her hadn’t diminished one whit. In fact, his hankering had blossomed and grown with the passing years. More than anything he wanted to drag Savannah to the floor and make love to her right there until they created a baby of their own as cute as Cody Markum.

Pipe dreams.

“In there,” she said gruffly, kicking the bathroom door open with the toe of her battered boot.

He shut the door behind him and turned on the water

faucet, remembering a time when Savannah would have been damned eager to keep him company. One particular incident rose to mind—the eve of his twenty-seventh birthday, just weeks before their breakup.

Sucking in a breath through clenched teeth, Matt splashed cold water on his face, attempting to chase away the haunting memory. Savannah and his friends had thrown him a party at the lake, and it was past midnight by the time they'd made it back to his apartment, damp and covered in sand, but kissing with unequaled fervency.

"Let's shower together," she'd whispered, tempting him beyond endurance by running a hand under his shirt and strumming his pebble-hard nipples.

Matt had almost made love to her that night. But despite his overheated passion, he'd managed to put on the brakes just in time. As much as he'd loved her, they'd had no protection, and he hadn't been willing to risk an unplanned pregnancy, not while he'd been waiting to hear if he'd gotten accepted into the specialized detective training in El Paso.

Besides, he'd wanted to wait until their wedding night to finally consummate their love. But *that* hadn't turned out the way he'd planned.

A sharp knock at the door broke his reverie.

"Are you setting up camp in there, Forrester?" Savannah asked.

"Just a minute."

Matt reached for a hand towel and mopped his face. Thinking about Savannah and that precious moment caused his body to harden. He stared at himself in the mirror. How had something so right ended so wrong?

He stepped out of the bathroom to find her tapping her toe impatiently. She brushed by him and slammed the door behind her. Perhaps he wasn't the only one reliving volatile memories.

"Matt," Ginger called to him as he returned to the kitchen. "Would you mind holding Cody? He keeps getting under my feet, and I'm scared I'll trip over him with a hot pan of grease or something."

"No problem." Matt smiled. He bent to scoop up the baby, who beamed and offered him a soggy teething cookie. "Hey there, big fella."

"Da!" Cody exclaimed.

"He calls everybody Da," Ginger explained quickly. "Even Savannah."

Matt cradled the squirming baby in the crook of his arm, overwhelmed by the sudden rush of emotion rolling through him. Cody smelled fresh and clean, like baby powder and sunshine. His hair stuck straight up on his head, a fuzzy brown halo.

"You look natural with a baby, Matt."

"What are you up to, Ginger? Don't be getting any crazy ideas."

Ginger shrugged. "She's still carrying a torch for you."

"Who? Savannah?" He snorted. "You've got to be kidding."

"Don't act like a big, dumb ape. Of course, Savannah."

"Yeah, right. She cared about me so much she rushed right out and married Gary Markum."

Ginger arched an eyebrow at him. "There's more to that story than you know."

"Oh." Matt leaned forward, hope knocking against him. "What are you talking about?"

"I mean," Ginger whispered, "she didn't have much choice."

"Ginger," Savannah said as she came into the room. "Don't burn the chicken." She'd changed into a pair of gray slacks and a white cotton blouse...and she'd put on lipstick.

For his benefit?

Matt's heart galloped like a racehorse on Derby Day. Was it true? Did Savannah still have feelings for him? The possibility tightened his gut with hope.

Savannah held out her arms toward Matt. "Give him to me."

Matt relinquished his hold on the child, his gaze searching Savannah's face.

She kept her eyes trained on Cody.

"Lunch is ready," Ginger said, dishing up the chicken. "You guys go ahead and start. I'll ring the dinner bell for Clem and Julio."

"Ah, yes," Matt said, "the elusive Mr. Diaz."

"Make yourself useful, Forrester. Set the table." Savannah settled Cody into his high chair and handed him a drumstick to gnaw on. "Plates are in the first cabinet on the left, silverware in the top drawer on your right."

"Running a ranch has given you a bossy streak, Savvy," he drawled, collecting the utensils.

"No," she replied coldly. "Growing up has made me assertive. I'm no longer the sweet little pushover you used to bulldoze so well."

Had he bulldozed her? He didn't remember it that way. If anything, she'd bulldozed him. He'd always been in awe of her, but now? He was completely blown away.

And that concerned him.

A big ol' heap of worry.

Around her he lost his grip on his professionalism and for a man who lived for his job, that was not a good thing.

Not good at all.

4

From her peripheral vision, Savannah watched Matt set the table. Surprisingly, he looked quite comfortable taking care of domestic chores. She wouldn't have thought it of him, considering his macho image. Two years ago, the man would have scoffed at the idea of doing woman's work. Obviously, she wasn't the only one who had changed.

Savannah set the platter of chicken on the table, followed it with a boat of cream gravy, mashed potatoes, and garden-fresh green beans. She lifted a pan of cornbread from the oven as Ginger came inside.

"Clem's coming, but I didn't see Julio." Ginger scratched her chin.

"Let's not wait for Julio, he'll be here soon." Savannah wanted the meal over and Matt out of her house.

"So, what's this I hear about you getting married?" Matt asked Ginger once they were seated around the kitchen table.

Ginger blushed. "Yep. May twenty-sixth."

"That's only two weeks away."

"Savannah's making my dress. It's gorgeous."

Matt raised an eyebrow. "I didn't know you could sew, Savvy."

She wished he'd stop calling her that. It brought back too many painful memories. "I can do a lot of things you don't know about, Matt."

"I don't doubt that."

Clem wandered in, washed his hands at the sink, and slipped into his place at the table without speaking. Savannah noticed he kept darting uneasy glances in Matt's direction.

"So, who's the lucky fella, Ginger?" Matt settled a napkin in his lap.

"Todd Baxter." She grinned.

"He's my insurance agent." Matt nodded. "A hard worker. I like him a lot."

Savannah watched them without commenting. The two had always been close. Ginger saw Matt as an older-brother figure. It had hurt Ginger almost as much as it had Savannah when she'd broken up with him.

"Can you come to the wedding, Matt?" Ginger asked. "I'd love to have you there."

"I appreciate the invitation, Ginger, but I can't make any promises. A detective's schedule can be unpredictable."

"I bet it's an exciting job, though." Ginger's eyes glowed.

"More boring than you'd think. Lots of paperwork."

"How often do you get in shootouts?"

"Very rarely." Matt was watching Savannah now.

She had told him she was breaking up with him because of his job. It was a good excuse. She hated knowing he could be killed on his job. But how could she ask him to quit it? She wouldn't be responsible for clipping his wings. That was true, too. He lived and breathed his work. It's who he was.

And then he'd actually gotten shot during that awful altercation over Jackie Spencer at Kelly's bar. Proving her point.

But she'd made love to him after he was released from the

hospital because she'd been so scared she was going to lose him. Then two days later, he asked her to marry him, bended knee, diamond ring and all, she'd had to turn him down. For an excuse, she'd said she couldn't wait around to become his widow. And when he told her how much he loved her, she'd forced herself not to say it back. Because she could not bear to reveal the real reason they could not be together. If he knew the real reason why, he would have given up everything for her, and simply she couldn't allow that. He would have insisted on staying with her no matter what. Which was precisely why she'd had to force him to go.

Savannah's heart broke all over again at the memory.

Ironically, she'd wound up a widow anyway. It seemed the men in her life were determined to leave her one way or the other.

Just like Pop.

After years of cheating on their mother, her father had abandoned the family when Savannah was seventeen. He'd disappeared a week after their mother's breast cancer diagnosis. His leaving had been a relief, actually. A welcomed respite from her parents' constant shouting matches.

Sitting here with him again, she was questioning her decisions. She'd made them in the heat of emotional tumult. But now? She had new decisions to make. Difficult decisions that would profoundly affect them both.

"You're not eating, Vannah. Something wrong with the food?" Ginger asked.

"No." Savannah stared at her untouched plate and forced herself to swallow a bite.

"It's delicious," Matt assured Ginger.

"Da!" Cody squealed and rubbed the drumstick across the top of his head as if agreeing with Matt.

"You are so adorable," Ginger gushed.

Cody dropped his drumstick on the floor and promptly burst into tears.

Glad for the distraction, Savannah pushed back her chair and got to her feet. “It’s naptime,” she declared and eased Cody from his high chair.

She carried her son into the front bedroom, her heart aching, heavy with memories. She wished Matt would leave. His being here brought back the tough choices she faced. Unfortunately, she needed his help. If the Santa Gertrudis were not recovered, she’d be in big trouble.

Cody fussed as she cleaned his face and hands with a washcloth. She reached for a diaper to change him and caught movement from the corner of her eye.

Matt.

He lounged against the doorframe, his pose insouciant. His arms were clasped loosely across his chest, one knee cocked at an incidental angle. But Savannah knew beneath the casual facade, he was tense, wary. A cautious law enforcement officer.

“We need to talk,” he said.

She shrugged, and concentrated on changing Cody, but her pulse quickened. “So talk.”

“I see no reason for us to keep tiptoeing around the past.” He moved closer.

“I’m not tiptoeing,” she denied.

“We’re not confronting it either.”

She turned to face him. “Why should we? What does it matter? Things were over between us a long time ago.”

“I was hoping maybe we could be friends.”

“I don’t think that’s wise.” She picked Cody up, and clutched him to her chest. “After all, you’re investigating the theft of my cattle. Isn’t that a conflict of interest or something?”

"After the investigation is over, of course." He edged another few steps in her direction.

"It wouldn't work." She gulped and stared at a bright-yellow wooden bunny painted on the nursery wall. It was time to change the nursery décor from infant to toddler. A firetruck theme? Or maybe horses. Matt would vote for the horses. Jeeze why was she thinking about what Matt would vote for?

Cody whimpered, squirming as if detecting her taut, stretched emotions.

Matt stood so near she could smell him. The familiar aroma stirred her. The scent of pure, masculine male—earthy, rich, delightful.

"I want you to know I've forgiven you," he said.

"Forgiven me? I did nothing that needed forgiving." Nothing he knew about anyway. But she wasn't opening that can of worms. Not yet. She had to figure out *if* she was going to break her vow to Gary and tell Matt that Cody was his son, and if so, when and how.

Cody threw back his head and squalled, huge tears collecting at the corners of his eyes.

"Here." Matt held out his hands. "Let me try to calm the little guy. I bet he misses his daddy."

Daddy.

Savannah froze at the word. Did Matt suspect something? Fear tinged her voice with anger. "Don't be ridiculous. He never even knew his father. Gary died when he was six weeks old."

"Every boy needs a man around."

"That's the key word, Matt. *Around.* Not a man who spends his time traipsing across the state after criminals. Not a man who likes mixing it up with outlaws in gun battles. Not a man who could wind up dead at any minute."

Matt gave her an odd look as if her reaction was totally over-the-top, which she supposed it was. "A man like Gary?"

"That's a low blow. Gary didn't go looking for cancer the way you court danger."

Why was she clinging to her old excuse? Why? Because there was nothing else to cling to.

She'd used his job as a reason to end their relationship and hadn't told him that she loved him too when he said the words to her.

Even though it was true that his dangerous job worried her, it wasn't the real reason she'd broken up with him.

How did she begin to tell him that she'd learned the day after they'd made love, that she carried the BRCA1 gene, and unless she had a radical bilateral mastectomy and had her ovaries removed, she would most likely die young from either breast or ovarian cancer?

She refused to allow Matt to sign on for that. She knew firsthand what it was like to watch someone you love die too young from cancer.

So she'd sent him away, because if he knew the truth, Matt would never have left her side. And she refused to put him through that hell. Her rationale at the time? As much as it hurt her to let him go, he deserved a wife who could give him children. A wife who could grow old with him.

Then three weeks after Matt left town for advanced training in El Paso, during a consultation with her doctor about undergoing prophylactic surgery that would take her breasts and her ovaries, she'd discovered she was pregnant with Cody.

She folded her arms across the breasts she'd had reconstructed following the mastectomies after she'd given birth to her son. It was all still new. The last surgery was only six months ago. If it hadn't been for Ginger, she didn't know how she would have gotten through the previous two years filled with so much sorrow and grief.

"I'm sorry, Savvy. I was way out of line with that comment," Matt said, snapping her back to the moment, back to the room with the three of them.

"Huh?" She blinked.

"Here, let me hold him." Matt clapped his hands, and Cody reached for him.

Savannah sucked in her breath.

Heartbroken, she watched Matt enfold their son to his chest. At that moment, the question she'd been debating for the past two years was answered. She *had* to tell him the baby was his. No matter what she'd promised Gary.

But how to break the news?

He walked across the room, settled into the rocking chair, and slowly began to rock. Savannah stared, incredulous. When they were dating, Matt had never expressed any interest in children. It surprised her to see him so at ease with Cody.

Seeing her son and his father together filled Savannah with a tumble of mixed emotions—awe, tenderness, regret, so much regret.

Her bottom lip quivered. This was ridiculous. Why would the sight of the big man cuddling the small boy make her want to cry? A sharp contrast between weak and strong. The protector nurturing the defenseless. Or was it because she was watching father and son bond for the first time?

Tell him. Tell him the baby is his.

Cody's eyelids drooped. Matt looked so comfortable, so self-assured in the role of father. Savannah turned her back on them as a single tear slid down her cheek.

Only the creaking chair disturbed the silence. Savannah fisted her hands as misery seeped through her bones. She'd made a lot of mistakes in her life, but falling in love with Matt was not one of them.

"I think he's asleep," Matt whispered.

"He's been up since six."

With slow, deliberate movements designed not to jar, Matt stood, edged to the crib, and softly laid Cody down and then changed his diaper. Cody's eyes opened but then drooped again, sleep claiming. Matt hesitated a moment, leaning over the crib, his gaze transfixed on the boy.

What he was thinking? Did he feel the brunt of regrets as severely as she? Did he have any inkling that the child was his?

Matt straightened and took Savannah's elbow. "Come on," he whispered, guiding her out into the hallway.

His grip burned her skin. Waves of heat radiated up her arm.

She twisted away from him, unable to bear the intensity of her body's reaction to his touch. Tossing her head, she rushed through the living room and into the kitchen. Found Ginger standing in front of the sink, washing dishes by hand. The dishwasher wasn't working, and Savannah couldn't afford a new one.

"Julio never showed up for lunch," her sister said. "So I saved him some chicken."

"I have a feeling you shouldn't have bothered," Matt said, following close behind Savannah.

"What do you mean?" Ginger asked.

"I think Mr. Diaz has some knowledge of what happened to your cattle. My guess is he's left the ranch."

"Julio?" Ginger raised her eyebrows in disbelief.

"He's probably just busy moving the herd." Savannah refused to believe Julio was involved. "I'll have Clem go look for him." Anxious to distance herself from Matt, she stepped outside and waved to Clem, who was wheeling the riding lawn mower around the front yard.

When he caught sight of her, the elderly man stopped the engine. "Need something, Miss Savannah?"

"Could you check the bunkhouse, see if Julio is washing up for lunch, Clem?"

"Sure thing."

The back door opened, and Matt joined her on the porch. "I still need Gary's records, if you can find them for me."

"I told you, nothing's missing besides the cattle."

"That's the kicker, Savannah."

"What do you mean?" she asked, squinting against the bright spring sunshine. A mockingbird trilled in a nearby mesquite tree. In the flower bed along the sidewalk, a row of cannas danced in the slight breeze.

"Something else *should* be missing."

Savannah lifted a hand to her throat. "And you suspect Julio?"

"I suspect everyone, Savvy. It's the nature of my job."

She caught his cold stare. "Do you suspect me, Matt?"

"Do I have a reason to?"

"You'll never change, will you?"

"What's that supposed to mean?"

"Your work will always be your first loyalty."

"That's right," he said, "*always*."

That's what she was afraid of. No woman could ever compete with the sheriff's department.

Butterflies chased around the milkweed. Bees hummed in the flowers. The luscious scent of honeysuckle wafted in the air. A beautiful afternoon. But Savannah couldn't enjoy it. The secret she kept knotted her up inside.

"You going to have Ginger's wedding here?" he asked.

"Yes," she answered, relieved he'd changed the subject.

He shook his head. "I can't believe it, our little Ginger getting married."

Our.

As if they were still together, still a couple. It was a beautiful word that stoked Savannah's regret. "She's twenty-one. Old enough."

"Would it disturb you if I came to the wedding?"

"Ginger invited you. It's her wedding."

"You didn't invite me to yours," he said lightly, resting an arm on the porch railing.

Savannah closed her eyes. How she'd wanted Matt to show up and stop the wedding. Save her. To rescue her from herself. When the minister had come to the part in the ceremony about anyone knowing why these two should not be married, Savannah had dreamed Matt would ride up on a white horse and exclaim, "She can't marry Gary. I love her!"

Of course, that stupid, girlish fantasy had been just that, a fantasy. She'd faced the hard facts. She married Gary because she'd been in trouble, and he was dying and needed someone as badly as she needed him.

Although everyone in Rascal knew Gary, she hadn't officially met him until she'd joined a cancer support group with her mother during her last few weeks of Mom's life. When Gary invited her out for coffee, he'd been so kind and understanding, and she'd found herself telling him about her pregnancy, and that's when he'd offered the solution.

Marry him, and he'd give her baby a name and a heritage. The Circle B would be Cody's one day. In exchange, Gary would get someone to nurse him through his final days. Although she'd had to promise that she would never reveal the truth that Cody wasn't Gary's baby. Ginger was the only one who knew.

She'd been desperate. What choice had she had?

Um, you could have told Matt the truth?

She'd almost told him. She'd found out where he was living, drove to El Paso and waited anxiously outside his apartment, trying to gather her courage. Then she'd seen him come home with a Jackie Spencer. The bartender from Kelly's that he'd gotten shot over. He'd led Jackie into his apartment and closed the door solidly behind them. It didn't take a genius to figure out what was going on behind closed doors.

That night, she'd gathered her resolve, vowed to keep her secret forever, and drove home to accept Gary's proposal.

"Savannah." His voice was low, husky. She opened her eyes and looked at him. Pure electricity surged in his gaze.

"Yes?"

"I'm so sorry."

"It doesn't matter." Not now. She'd set her heart against romantic love, had settled for comfort and convenience, had gone forward with her life.

"Look." Matt pointed at Clem.

The old ranch hand came loping across the field. "Miss Savannah! Miss Savannah!"

Savannah and Matt left the porch and met him in the middle of the yard. "What's the matter, Clem?" she asked, but she already knew the answer.

"It's Julio," Clem rasped, hitching in ragged breaths. He clasped a hand to his side.

"What?" Matt demanded.

"He's gone. Cleared out. Even took the sheets off his bunk."

5

Matt mentally kicked himself for wasting time arguing with Savannah when he should have been tracking Julio Diaz. Why couldn't he just forget her? There were plenty of other females eager to be with him. Why was he mooning over someone who apparently wanted nothing to do with him?

"Because you're a sentimental fool, Forrester," he growled and frowned at himself in the rearview mirror.

He couldn't forget how wonderful it had felt rocking Savannah's baby in his arms, pretending it was their child.

He had to get a grip. These daydreams would only bring heartache. Too much unresolved conflict existed between him and Savannah for them to ever have a future together.

Savannah was right about one thing, though. Being a sheriff's detective wasn't a career for a family man. It required too much time on the road and involved too much danger.

Yet, he loved his job. Had known it was his calling from the tender age of twelve when his family had lost their farm. The old memory floated through his mind like a whiff of acrid wood smoke. Like most peanut farmers in West Texas, his dad had mortgaged the homestead to the hilt, banking on a bumper crop of peanuts to rescue them from debt.

But that year, Matt's grandmother died, and the whole family departed on a week-long trip to California.

They'd returned home to discover their fields stripped bare. The peanut crop had been harvested by thieves. The bank ended up foreclosed on the farm, Matt's family ended up living with his uncle and aunt, and the crooks went free. From that day on, Matt swore revenge, if not on those particular thieves then on any others who dared to prey on the innocent, hardworking folks of Texas. And so began his journey in law enforcement, doing what he loved best—bringing the wicked to justice.

That was something Savvy just didn't understand.

Women. Once they got tangled up in a guy's mind, they could distract the most dedicated lawman.

Still, it was no excuse.

He knew better than to let anything interfere with an investigation. He wheeled his Jeep down the highway, heading for the border and Mexico if necessary. He'd lifted Julio's prints from the bunkhouse, run them through the computer, and discovered that Diaz was an undocumented worker from Nuevo Laredo.

And quite possibly a cattle thief.

From now on, he'd keep his head focused on his job where it belonged. The past was dead. Buried with his youthful fantasies of a wife, kids, and a loyal dog to return home to at the end of each day.

Satisfied he'd made the right decision despite the hurt ricocheting inside him, Matt trod heavily on the accelerator and sped away into the dark West Texas night.

Savannah worried.

It had been a week since Matt had left the ranch to go looking for Julio Diaz.

Where was he?

She fretted. Had something happened? Had he found Julio? A dozen possible scenarios floated through her mind, each more alarming than the one before. Why hadn't he let her know something by now? Had he been hurt?

Or worse?

She tried texting his old phone number, but it was no longer in service, and he hadn't given her his new one. Finally, too anxious to stand the suspense any longer, she gathered her courage and called the sheriff. The dispatcher who answered listened sympathetically but hadn't been able to give her much information. The woman had, however, told Savannah that Matt wasn't in Rascal.

"Forrester, where are you?" Savannah sighed.

She looked into the brilliant blue sky, rocked back on her heels, tossed a handful of weeds into a pile, and peeled off her gardening gloves. With Julio gone, more of the ranching chores had fallen on her shoulders, leaving her precious little time to prepare for the wedding. Luckily, Ginger's fiancé, Todd, had volunteered to help get the garden ready for the ceremony on Saturday.

"Did you say something, Savannah?" Todd asked, resting one well-muscled arm on his shovel and swiping the other arm across his damp forehead.

"Thinking out loud." Savannah shook her head.

"Where do you want these geraniums?" Ginger asked, carrying an armful of the colorful blooms in a clay pot.

"Along the path." Savannah got to her feet and pointed with a trowel.

"Da!" Cody hollered from his Pack 'n Play underneath the shady mimosa tree Savannah had planted to honor Gary's life.

Todd squinted at the horizon. "Looks like we got company."

"Oh?" Savannah followed his gaze.

Dust billowed in the distance, and through it, she saw a flash of red. Matt's Jeep? Instant relief splashed across her heart. Don't be ridiculous, Savannah scolded herself, a red vehicle did not necessarily mean it was Matt.

"Good time to take a break." She planted her palms in the small of her back. "Anybody up for lemonade?"

"Sounds mighty fine," Todd agreed.

"Me, too," Ginger added, setting down the geraniums.

"Drinks all around then."

From the corner of her eye, Savannah saw Todd lean over and plant a kiss on Ginger's eager lips. A sliver of envy sliced through her. Oh, to be that young and that in love again.

She went into the house and washed her hands. She retrieved a pitcher of fresh-squeezed lemonade from the refrigerator, iced down four glasses, arranged everything on a tray, and stepped outside just as Matt's red Jeep pulled into the driveway.

It's him! She thought giddily. *If only I could fling myself into his arms!* But instead, she set the lemonade down on the picnic table and waited for him to join them.

As he drew near, her heart hammered. The tan Stetson hid his face. His shoulders swayed as he swaggered across the yard, looking for all the world like the hero in an old-fashioned Western. Affection vaulted into her throat at the sight of him.

"Afternoon, Ginger, Todd, Savannah," he greeted, doffing his hat.

"Hello, Matt," Savannah said.

To her dismay, she noticed a fresh cut traveled from Matt's right brow down his cheekbone. Five neat, black stitches knitted the wound. Her hand flew to her throat, and she sucked in a breath. He'd been hurt!

"Hi." Ginger raised a hand. "We were about to have some lemonade. Care to join us?"

"Sounds good." He ran a hand through his hair. Savannah could feel the heat of his gaze on her face. She longed to ask him how he'd earned that gash.

Matt eased himself down on the patio chair as if his whole body ached from the effort of moving. He'd been in a fight.

"Getting ready for the wedding?" Matt nodded at the freshly tended flower garden.

"Yeah." Ginger beamed, pouring lemonade while Todd sat down next to Matt. "Only a week away. I can't wait."

"What happened to your face?" Todd asked bluntly. Ginger nestled next to her husband-to-be and Todd slid an arm around her waist.

"You mean this?" Matt pointed at the scar. "This is nothing." He looked at Savannah as if weighing her response.

Savannah wrapped her fingers around her glass. She yearned to reach out and comfort him, soothe his pain, yet she knew acting on those feelings would land her in a world of hurt.

"Have a seat," Matt invited, patting the spot beside him.

"I'm fine right here." Savannah leaned against the mimosa's trunk and placing the sole of one foot flat against the tree's bark.

"Did you catch up with Julio?" Ginger asked.

"Yep." Matt nodded, and took another long drink of lemonade.

"And?" Savannah stared at him and raised her eyebrows.

"Julio's not a cattle thief, but he does have a way with a switchblade knife." Matt gingerly fingered the cut.

Wincing, Savannah grit her teeth. "Julio did that to you?" She felt sick at the thought.

"That hombre didn't take too kindly to being arrested."

"I can't believe you're treating this so lightly," Savannah said.

The same emotions she'd experienced so vividly two years ago roiled through her, as raw and as fresh as before. She recalled the night in Kelly's bar when that drunken cowpoke had started a brawl with another guy over a Jackie Spencer. Matt hadn't known the cowpoke carried a tiny pistol in his boot and when Matt had gotten in the middle of things to break up the fight, his had earned him a bullet in the arm and started the chain of events that had led them to his moment.

"Julio didn't steal the cattle?" Savannah set her glass on the table.

"Nope." Matt sent her a cocky grin.

"So?" She raised her palms. "Why did Julio run if he wasn't involved in the thefts?"

"No mystery. Julio thought I was from immigration. My Spanish is limited, and his English is worse. We tussled before we started communicating." Matt indicated his wound.

How could he remain so unflustered after having his cheek filleted?

"Actually, Julio turned out to be pretty cooperative once we got better acquainted." Matt tipped back on the legs of his chair, balancing his weight perfectly, and teased her with a mocking smile.

"Is that what you've been doing the last week? Tracking Julio?" Savannah asked, folding her arms across her chest.

"Among other things."

"What about my cattle?"

"Haven't seen hide nor hair of 'em."

Savannah glanced over to find Todd and Ginger wrapped in the throes of a passionate embrace. Heat raced up her neck when Matt caught the direction of her gaze. She inclined her head toward the barn. "Let's take a walk."

"Thought you'd never ask."

She started across the yard, Matt right behind her.

"Think they'll even notice we're gone?" Matt whispered, so close the warmth of his breath tickled her ear.

"Those two had better get married soon, or I'll be forced to get out the water hose," Savannah said wryly once they were out of sight.

"We used to be worse than they are. Remember, Savvy?"

Her blush deepened, and she stopped walking when they reached the barnyard. "We're not foolish kids anymore, Matt."

"You remember our first date?" He leaned one shoulder casually against the side of the barn. Reaching over, he lifted a strand of hair from her shoulder and rolled it between his fingers.

Savannah inhaled sharply.

Their eyes met.

"Do you remember, Savvy?" he repeated.

She swallowed. "Yes."

Boy, did she ever. How could she forget the powerful energy of their first explosive kiss during that hayride at his uncle's farm? She'd been ready to surrender herself to him at the end of that night. The memory forced her to drop her gaze.

He swung his Stetson between a thumb and index finger with slow, calculated movements, as if fanning a flame. "Do you remember going back to my place?" His voice had lowered to a deep purr.

"Uh-huh," she whispered.

"I played my guitar for you."

"I remember. 'The Twelfth of Never.'"

His magnetic eyes held her hypnotized. "We talked about everything under the sun."

"I know."

"And at midnight ordered a pepperoni and mushroom pizza to go just as Speedy's Pizza was closing."

"We ate it cold because we couldn't stop kissing," she finished.

Tingles radiated from her inside out—steamy, melting, erotic. Paralyzed, Savannah drifted on the memories. Matt, his arms around her, strong and sure. Matt, his lips on hers, soft and tender. Matt, the man himself, so honest, so sincere. She'd known he would always keep her safe, would never hurt her.

At least not intentionally.

She'd been the one to hurt him. Not that she'd really had much choice.

"Do you remember what you asked me, about four in the morning?" His voice turned husky, dry with emotion.

"I... I... asked if I could stay the night with you."

"That's right." His smile deepened. He leaned forward, cupping a finger under her chin, and tipping her head back until she was forced to look him in the eyes. "What was my answer?"

Her knees wobbled, and Savannah feared her legs might fold.

She cleared her throat and laced her fingers together. His touch burned hotter than a branding iron. "You said no, that we should wait." She hesitated. "You told me I was too special to take lightly."

"You're still special to me, Savvy."

Her gaze, restless and hungry, wandered over his face. She'd dreamed of this dear face for so long—his sun-browned forehead, his slightly crooked nose, his firm, full lips curling easily into a teasing grin, the slight crinkles etched into the corners of his dark eyes.

And that fresh, jagged scar.

Savannah jerked back, dropping her gaze. The ugly scar

reminded her of the things that stood between them—his thirst for daring adventure, his lack of fear, his need to prove his manhood with fists and weapons, the frustrating way women threw themselves at him. The lies she'd told. The secrets she kept.

He'd chosen the right career for his personality. He was a brave man, a stalwart one. A good man. A man who deserved to know his son.

"Savvy?" he rasped.

Her heart strummed steadily, blood whooshing in her ears with each beat. Was this the time to tell Matt about Cody? How did she start the conversation? Savannah cleared her throat, trying to find the words.

"I'm sorry about Gary," he said.

"Me, too."

"Although I was jealous of him, I never wished him ill."

"I know."

"It must have been hard for you." The touch of sympathy in his voice grated on her. "Losing your mom, then Gary less than a year afterward."

"Life can be hard." She twisted her shoulder. She knew she sounded tough, cynical, but if she allowed in those tender feelings, she'd break down.

"I've missed having you in my life, Savvy."

"I missed you, too." Her voice cracked, broke.

"I'd forgotten how your eyes turn to liquid gold when you're deep in thought," he said, leaning closer and angling his head downward.

Instinct hollered for her to pull back, to run away, but for once she listened to her heart and stayed rooted to the sandy earth, waiting.

Cicadas buzzed in the mesquite tree. A trickle of sweat dampened the back of her neck. She looked into Matt's shimmering dark-eyed gaze, found herself trapped there like a bug in a spider's web. She moistened her lips with her tongue.

"Savannah," he whispered.

"Yes?" she whispered back.

He kissed her.

6

His mouth covered hers—hungry, searching. His Stetson dropped to the ground as his arms encircled her shoulders, and he pulled her tight against his chest.

This isn't prudent. She should squirm free so she could tell him what she needed to tell him, but she had no inclination to resist. She wanted only to float in the pleasure.

His heated tongue requested entrance past the barrier of her teeth. His eager fingers stroked her throat. He growled low and insistent, the rough, masculine sound igniting a wildfire deep in the recesses of her aching abdomen.

"Oh, Savvy," he exclaimed, letting go of her just long enough to breathe in a gulp of air. "It's been too long."

She surrendered. Fully, unconditionally, without a fight.

Her weak body was as starved for him as he was for her. She tilted her head back to give him easier access, welcoming his tender invasion, heralding his long-anticipated return, savoring his delicious taste—a provocative combination of peppermint and lemonade.

A dizzy giddiness swept through her. Time halted,

reversed. She felt twenty-three again—young, ripe, ready for his loving.

Her fingers threaded through his hair as she tugged his head down, down. How had she survived without him, without this, for two lonely years? Unshed tears collected in her throat. She'd made so many mistakes.

One of Matt's hands slipped beneath her blouse, caressed her bare stomach.

Torture, pure torture. She wanted him so desperately, yet she knew she couldn't have him. Not until she told him the truth, and when she revealed her secret, would he still want her?

Savannah moaned.

A sound pricked her ears. A muffled whimper, then a full-blown cry.

Cody.

She placed both hands on Matt's chest and pushed. "No."

Matt blinked, disoriented as if he'd been dragged from a heavenly dream into the harsh reality of daylight. "What is it?" he rasped, his dark hair askew.

"Cody." She hurried toward the playpen.

Bending over, she picked up her son, *their* son, and tried to ignore the throbbing of her kiss-blistered lips.

Matt came up behind her. "Savvy?"

She refused to turn around. If she met his gaze, she feared she might burst into tears.

"I'm sorry, I was completely out of line," he said.

She shook her head, unable to speak. No, she'd been the one out of line. She should have told him about his son when she'd first got pregnant. But he'd been gone, and her mother was so sick, and Gary had been there, offering her comfort and support. And when she *had* gone to see him, he'd been with Jackie Spencer.

"I didn't come here to kiss you."

"I know," she squeaked. "It just happened. We best forget it."

❧

Matt stuck his hands in his front pockets and focused his attention on the tips of his boots. Why had he succumbed to the temptation of her full, lush mouth? He'd sworn he wouldn't kiss her again and look what had happened. He was a law enforcement officer. He'd been taught strength, restraint, self-control, yet one look into Savannah's gold-green eyes, and he'd crumbled like a cookie in a glass of warm milk.

Dammit.

He yearned to comfort her, to tell her everything was going to be all right, but they weren't kids anymore. They both knew such words smacked of mindless platitudes. Life just didn't work that way.

"Savannah, if you could get me Gary's ranching records, I'll conclude my business and be on my way."

She nodded and held her shoulders stiff. "They're in the house. In Gary's desk."

He followed her, feeling woefully inept. They needed to talk, but Matt could not adequately articulate his feelings.

What had he expected when he'd kissed her? That she would ask him to take her back? That she would renounce her past mistakes, beg his forgiveness, tell him she loved him?

He snorted. Fairytales.

Cody smiled at him over Savannah's shoulder. Such a cute kid. That grin affected him viscerally. Like a penny dropped into a bottomless well, Matt felt himself falling for the little scamp.

Matt grinned back, his spirits buoyed.

Savannah led Matt to a bedroom in the back of the house.

He glared at the queen-size bed in the corner. Was this the bed she'd shared with Markum? Was this where they'd created Cody? That thought exploded in Matt's mind like a rocket blast.

Why was he torturing himself? Forcefully, he pried his gaze from the quilt-covered bed to the slender young woman standing in front of him.

She burrowed through a scarred, antique, roll-top desk sitting off to one side. It was piled high with scraps of paper.

"I'm afraid it's a mess." Savannah cradled Cody's head in her palm. "I even filed for an extension on my income tax because I couldn't summon the courage to go through it."

She sounded sad. Matt swallowed hard. Had she really loved Gary? Or had she married him on the rebound? Had she experienced with Gary the same wild passion he and she once shared?

His gaze strayed to the third finger of her left hand. Unexpected joy floated through him. Her ring finger was bare. She'd stopped wearing her wedding band.

Savannah stepped to the desk, her gently swaying hips causing a stir inside Matt. He had to stop this agonizing self-torture. Averting his gaze, he forced his mind onto the investigation and reviewed the evidence while he waited for her to find the papers.

One—his prime suspect, Julio Diaz, had been exonerated.

Two—he'd arrested the three men in San Antonio accused of stealing Kurt McNally's belt buckle, and they'd readily confessed to robbing the other five ranches, but all four denied knowing anything about the missing Santa Gertrudis herd at the Circle B.

Three—two local scumbags, Brent Larkins and Hootie Thompson, had been slinging money around Kelly's and bragging about their sudden wealth. Although the two men might not have burglarized the Circle B, Matt's instincts told him they'd been up to no good.

Four—some unknown Santa Gertrudis cattle had turned up in Midland with their brands altered.

"I think this is what you need." Savannah's voice broke into his thoughts as she handed him a thick manila folder.

"Thank you," he said, fingering the brim of his Stetson.

"You'll let me know when you hear something about my cattle?"

He nodded. "Of course."

Matt stood there, feeling awkward. Savannah studied her son, evidently as discombobulated as he.

"Listen," they both said at once.

"Go ahead." Savannah emitted a nervous chuckle. "You first."

"I'm sorry about that kiss."

"Are you really?"

"No."

"Me, either," she said, giving him a shy grin from beneath lowered lashes.

At her words, he felt like a helium balloon let loose to soar into the clouds—free, unfettered, floaty. Did he stand a chance of winning her back?

Cody, his face nestled against Savannah's breast, peeked sideways at Matt.

"Thanks for the paperwork." He held up the manila folder. "I'll return it as soon as I can."

"No hurry."

Savannah walked him to the front door, his heart pounding with the remembered promise of her soft lips. Common sense told him to proceed with caution, but something stronger, something intense, tempted him to throw discretion to the wind.

To keep from saying more than he should, Matt turned without a backward glance, got into his Jeep, and drove away.

Wanting to touch base with his most reliable contact, Matt stopped by Kelly's on the way home. The heavy wooden door creaked in protest as Matt walked into the smoky room. He blinked, letting his eyes adjust to the darkened interior.

"Hey, Jimbo." He waved at the bartender and plopped down on a stool. At four o'clock in the afternoon, the place was almost deserted.

"What'll you have, Detective Forrester?" Jim placed a napkin on the bar in front of Matt.

"Water will do me just fine. And a little information."

"I'm beginning to think you only come in here to pump me for secrets," Jim said, filling a glass with ice and water from the tap.

Matt narrowed his gaze and stared at the two men at a corner table, hunched down in their chairs, their eyes trained on their beers. Brent Larkins and Hootie Thompson.

"Those two been around a lot lately?" Matt asked Jim, inclining his head in the direction of the unsavory duo.

Brent's and Hootie's rap sheets went way back to adolescence for shoplifting. They'd graduated to hot-wiring cars, illegal gambling, fencing stolen goods, and had eventually moved on to breaking and entering. Both had done a series of short stints at the state prison in Huntsville.

Jim nodded as he polished water spots from a glass with a hand towel. "And throwing lots of money around."

"Any explanation for it?"

"Claimed they won a bundle on the ponies last Saturday."

Matt ran a hand along his five o'clock shadow. Time to have a talk with Rascal's resident thugs. He picked up his water glass, thrust out his chest, and sauntered over to their table.

"Howdy, fellas," he greeted, pulling up a chair.

Hootie grunted and pulled a red cocktail straw through his unattractive teeth. Something about the gesture tugged at Matt's memory.

"Whatcha want?" Larkins snarled, a trail of beer foam clinging to his scraggly mustache.

"I hear tell you men found yourselves some extra cash." Matt kept his eyes on them. These two had a reputation for carrying concealed weapons. Matt noticed three mugs and at least a dozen empty beer bottles cluttering the table. Who had been keeping them company?

"Yeah," Larkins challenged. "We scored big at the track last week. That ain't illegal yet, is it?"

Hootie hee-hawed like a donkey and continued chewing the straw.

"I don't suppose you two know anything about the cattle thefts out at the Circle B, do you?" Matt arched an eyebrow.

Brent Larkins made a face. "Why, Detective, are you accusing us of something?"

"Not at all. Just thought you might have some information."

"We didn't even know about it." Larkins's dirty fingers curled around his beer mug. "Till just now."

The door to the nearby men's room opened, and an old man stumbled out. Matt looked up to see Clement Olson swaying in the doorway, his eyes rounding in surprise when he spotted Matt.

"Hello, Clem," Matt greeted him, a bad feeling snaking through his gut. This whole situation smelled mighty fishy. What was Savannah's hired hand doing drinking with riffraff like Larkins and Thompson?

Clem stood frozen for a second. Then suddenly he bolted for the front door.

"Aw, hell," Matt swore, getting to his feet and taking off

after Clem. He pushed outside in time to see Clem disappear behind the Dairy Diner next door.

"Clem," Matt shouted, sprinting to catch up to the panicky old man. "Wait."

Clem halted next to a trash Dumpster. His whole body trembled as he raised both palms defensively. "I didn't do nothing!"

"I just want to talk to you, Clem. What were you doing hanging out with those two?" Matt stepped closer, adopting a tough stance, feet wide apart, hands on his hips.

"They bought me a beer." Clem wheezed, slightly short of breath.

"Is that all?"

Clem hung his head. "Yeah."

"Savannah know you're here?"

"No. You won't tell her, will you?"

Matt sighed. "Only if you promise to go home and quit wasting your time hanging around those two."

"I swear it."

Placing his hand on Clem's shoulder, Matt squeezed firmly. "See that you do."

"I will. I promise."

As he walked back to his Jeep, Matt turned the events over in his mind. The whole thing was suspicious. Clem passing the time of day with Larkins and Thompson. The old man worked for Savannah, and her livestock had come up missing at a time when cattle were conveniently disappearing all over the county. Hootie Thompson liked to chew up red cocktail straws, and Matt had found such a straw at the scene of the thefts. Matt didn't like the scenario one bit. What he needed now, however, was solid evidence.

Gary Markum's papers might hold the key. That and the Santa Gertrudis cattle with the altered brands that had turned up in Midland.

He sat in his Jeep, watching Clem meander back into the bar. Rolling his window down for air, Matt sighed. He picked up the manila folder and leafed through it. Gary Markum's leisurely scrawl recorded cattle purchases, weather reports, feed bills.

Branding records, that's what he needed. Something, anything to tie Clem, Larkins, and Thompson to the thefts. Matt kept searching.

Vaccination lists, calving times, notes on fencing repairs. He dampened his fingertip with the tip of his tongue, flipped the pages quicker. Invoices, bank statements, an insurance policy.

Insurance policy?

He extracted the six-page document underwritten by Texas Farmers Insurance, Todd Baxter, agent. A tight knot wadded in his throat as he clutched the paper in his fists. What he read sickened him.

Suddenly everything made an ugly, logical kind of sense.

A seventy-five-thousand-dollar insurance policy issued for twenty-four head of purebred Santa Gertrudis cattle.

Listed as sole beneficiary was one Savannah Markum.

7

Ginger's wedding day arrived on a blast of pre-summer air—warm, sultry, and bursting with sunshine. Savannah whispered a prayer of thanks for the sunshine. From her own experience, outdoor weddings had a tendency to conjure thunderstorms.

Savannah had risen two hours earlier than usual to complete any last-minute preparations, only to find Ginger already awake, brewing a pot of coffee and pacing the kitchen floor.

"Couldn't sleep," she told Savannah with a sheepish grin. "This is more nerve-racking than Christmas Eve. Were you this nervous when you married Gary?"

Don't judge your wedding by mine, Savannah thought.

The congenial feelings she'd had for Gary couldn't be compared to the bright, shining love Todd and Ginger shared. Savannah merely nodded, poured herself a cup of coffee, and sat down at the kitchen table. She didn't want to remember the day she'd stopped believing that true love really could conquer all.

From the baby monitor on the table, they heard Cody wail.

"I'll go get him," Ginger said before Savannah could push back her chair. "I need something to do."

Closing her eyes, Savannah sighed, lifted her cup to her mouth, and sipped. Mentally, she reviewed the numerous tasks needing her attention before the four p.m. wedding. Direct the florist and the caterers, steam Ginger's dress, make sure Clem had the parking situation under control, attend to her own hair and nails, dress Cody.

Whew.

"Look who's awake," Ginger cooed, coming back into the room.

Savannah opened her eyes and grinned at her son. His fuzzy, brown hair stood straight up; his white cotton sleep shirt was molded to his chubby little torso. Cody reached for her, his smile glowing like a thousand-watt bulb. Gathering his familiar weight to her chest, Savannah breathed in her son's wonderful aroma. Cody could soothe her like nothing else on earth.

"Da!" he exclaimed and wrapped his arms around her neck.

Ginger's eyes misted. "I can't wait until Todd, and I have a baby of our own."

Savannah made a face. "Wait. You're only twenty-one. Lots of time for babies."

"Come on, Vannah, don't give me that. You adore Cody."

"Of course I do, but you and Todd need some time alone to get to know one another. With children come responsibilities. Enjoy each other for a while. Anytime you feel that maternal hunger, come borrow this little pistol for a day."

"Da." Cody nodded his head as if agreeing.

"I bet you're ready for breakfast, aren't you, son?" Savannah tickled his tummy.

Ginger clenched her fists. A large tear rolled down her cheek.

"Ginger, honey, what's wrong?" Savannah reached over and touched her sister's shoulder.

"I... I..." She gulped. "I'm going to miss you and Cody so much."

"Oh, is that all." Savannah waved a hand. She knew on a day like today Ginger's emotions were bound to take a few dips and turns. "I thought maybe you were having second thoughts about Todd."

"Oh, no. Never. I love Todd with all my heart."

"Good. That's the way it should be."

"Is that how it was between you and Gary?"

Savannah got up and settled Cody into his high chair. She kept her face hidden from her sister. "Gary was a good man."

"But you didn't love him like you loved Matt."

"Not all of us get a fairytale, Gin."

"But Matt's back now, and you're single again..."

"Stop trying to play matchmaker."

Opening the cabinets, Savannah took out a packet of instant cereal and mixed it with hot water. She refused to think about the past and Matt. This hectic day would require all her attention. She had neither the time nor the energy to waste on regrets. Or on wondering what might have been.

❧

MATT HAD POSTPONED THE INEVITABLE FOR TWO DAYS. Another case kept him occupied, but the whole time, his thoughts returned to Savannah like a tongue probing an abscessed tooth.

Was it possible that Savannah could be involved in an insurance fraud? He didn't want to believe she was capable of such a thing, but the facts stood out bold and undeniable.

One—her thefts were not related to the other thefts in the county. Two—her late husband had taken out a large policy on just those purebred Santa Gertrudis cattle. None of the other livestock at the Circle B had been insured. Three—Savannah was the sole beneficiary. Four—her ranch hand had been seen consorting with known criminals. Five—part of her herd had been located in Midland, their brands altered. Six—if Savannah had married Markum for his money, who was to say how low she might stoop for financial gain?

Matt swore under his breath. He stood at the kitchen sink where he'd just wolfed down a sausage biscuit. Dusting his fingers on a paper towel, he stared out the window, his mind lost in thought.

For two days, he'd tried to find some other explanation for the disappearance of the Santa Gertrudis herd, but all the evidence pointed to a certain honey-haired lady rancher.

Except two things didn't jibe. Why hadn't she contacted the insurance company about the loss? Was she cagey enough to wait? Had the recent thefts in the area sparked the idea in the first place?

And why had Savannah given him a copy of the insurance policy with Gary's papers? Had she been trying to confess?

Matt didn't know. Once he thought he'd understood her so well, but that had been two years ago before she'd broken up him without a rational explanation and married Markum on the rebound.

Matt sighed. No getting around it, he had to bring her in for questioning.

He drank the glass of milk, turned off the radio, lifted his Stetson off the hat rack, and plunked it down on his head. Like it or not, he and Savannah were overdue for a confrontation.

A dense knot rode in his chest during the twenty-mile trek to her ranch. Despite his best efforts to the contrary, he couldn't stop thinking about their past. He kept recalling her youthful enthusiasm, her natural exuberance for life, which had evaporated over two years. Instead of the eager, spontaneous girl he remembered, Matt had discovered a cautious, reserved young woman.

Until he kissed her.

The memory of the kiss they'd shared in the barnyard reignited buried feelings. When he kissed Savannah time had dissolved. Disappeared. It was as if they'd been transported back to his uncle's farm and the very first moment they'd kissed.

For those brief, precious seconds, Matt had felt that maybe, just maybe a chance existed that they might reconstruct the shattered pieces of their relationship. But after the kiss had ended, reality trampled that illusion. She'd broken his heart once, and he wasn't stupid enough to give her another opportunity. Especially if she was dealing in something as nefarious as insurance fraud.

What had happened to the sweet, naive Savannah Prentiss he'd once known?

It was nine a.m. when he turned into the driveway of the Circle B. Startled by the brightly colored canopies stretched out over the lawn, Matt stared at the folding metal chairs lined in neat rows underneath. He frowned wondering what was going on, and then he remembered.

Ginger's wedding.

He groaned. What lousy timing. How could he take Savannah in for questioning today? Yet, how could he not? He'd already delayed as long as he could, and he was feeling the heat from the sheriff.

"Bring Savannah Markum in," Sheriff Langley had growled at him last night before Matt left the office. "First thing tomorrow. If you're not comfortable conducting the questioning, someone else will handle it."

So here he was with orders to detain her and the desire to do just the opposite. Did he genuinely believe Savannah had plotted to have her own cattle stolen for the insurance? In his heart, no, but the matter demanded attention. He hated to be suspicious of her, but he had no choice, and Matt was nothing if not thorough.

He got out and adjusted his Stetson. Walking around the vehicles—Savannah's compact car, a pickup truck, a florist's van, two luxury cars—Matt made his way up the wide, sweeping drive.

Like any lawman worth his salt, he scanned his surroundings, noting every nuance, drawing conclusions based on his observations. Wedding day preparations and nothing more.

And then he caught the flash of movement from behind the barn.

He turned his head for a better glimpse and saw Clem Olson stumbling across the field in his haste to reach the bunkhouse. Matt's brow furrowed as he ran a hand along his jaw. He didn't trust the old man.

"Matt!"

He swung around to find Ginger standing on the back porch. She waved.

For the time being, he dismissed Clem and focused his attention on Savannah's little sister. He could remember when Ginger had worn braces and pigtails, and now she was getting married. She used to tag along after him and Savannah like an overzealous puppy. Matt smiled, recalling the numerous ploys they'd used to give her the slip.

"You came." Ginger dashed down the steps to wrap her arms around his waist. "I hoped you'd make it."

Guilt pressed down on Matt like a leaden ballast. He'd totally forgotten about Ginger's wedding.

"Wouldn't miss it for the world." He gently chucked her chin.

"I'm so glad you got here early. Maybe you could calm Savannah down. She drank a whole pot of coffee this morning, and now she's zooming around the house like an idling jet engine, making a lot of noise but not getting much done."

"Nervous, is she?" Matt grinned.

"Boy, is she ever." Ginger shook her head ruefully. "You'd think it was her wedding day."

Savannah had already had her wedding day, Matt thought. A cloud floated past the sun. The courtyard darkened. He remembered that day. How could he forget the moment when his world had come to a crashing halt? The day *his* girl had said "I do" to a middle-aged rancher. Matt clenched his jaw at the memory.

The screen door creaked open. He looked up to see Savannah standing in the doorway, her honey-colored hair caught back in a bright-blue bow, her long, tanned legs highlighted in a pair of white shorts.

He swallowed hard. No matter how he tried to fight it, the woman still possessed the power to transform his insides into mush. But he didn't have to let her know the influence she wielded over him.

"Hello, Matthew," she said, her voice as soft and cool as the sudden breeze.

"Savannah." He tipped his hat.

"I'm glad you were able to take time from your busy schedule to attend Ginger's wedding. It means a lot to her."

Was that a dig? He squinted. She kept her face expressionless. What thoughts churned behind those mesmerizing green-gold eyes? Did his presence disturb her? Did she fear he'd uncovered her scheme to defraud the insurance company?

That idea made him wince.

He wanted so badly to believe she wasn't capable of such a thing, but the truth was, he just didn't know her anymore.

And he hadn't understood her since that moment two years ago when she'd broken things off with him after they'd made love and he'd asked her to marry him. She'd said it was because of his job. Because he'd gotten shot. Because he was reckless.

No. Unless she was a superb actress, Savannah had once cared intensely for him. Matt prided himself on his judgment. It had rescued him from more than one jam during his career, but a person could change a lot over two years.

Who had Savannah become?

"YOU'RE HERE AWFULLY EARLY," SAVANNAH SAID, HER GAZE traveling the length of his body.

He wore a maroon-and-dark-green, snap-down Western shirt and a pair of new, sharply creased blue jeans. Not exactly wedding attire, but nothing unusual in this neck of the woods. For a casual outdoor wedding, West Texas informal would pass. Especially when worn by a man as potently masculine as Matt Forrester. His clothing made a statement, proclaiming him a rough, tough cowboy detective.

His dark eyes seized her gaze and held her captive. Savannah wanted to look away, but she couldn't. Helplessly, she stared at him. Her heart leaped in her chest like a jackrabbit trying to escape a snare. One look, one smile from him and she melted like ice cream in the sun.

"He came to help out." Ginger beamed. "Didn't I tell you he would show up?"

"I'll do anything I can to assist," Matt said. "Just tell me what to do."

Savannah nodded. "All right. I accept your offer. I need some tables brought out of the house and set up in the garden before the caterers arrive. I can't move them all by myself, and Clem seems to have disappeared."

"Lead the way."

They all went inside, Ginger flitting off to the bathroom to wash and flat iron her hair. Cody sat in his playpen in the living room, busily stacking alphabet blocks. He saw Matt and grinned, a string of drool dribbling down his chin.

"Da!" he squealed happily, wriggling with delight.

Savannah stopped to wipe her son's mouth with a corner of his baby blanket, then pointed out a table to Matt. "Let's move this one first. It's the heaviest."

They tugged the table out the door and into the garden where Savannah had him place it strategically beside the flower bed. The florists brought in colorful bouquets of spring flowers and arranged them around the constructed altar.

Savannah stopped to admire their handiwork. The setup was quite attractive. She couldn't help but compare the elaborate decorations to her own slipshod, hurry-up wedding. There had been no florists, only artificial flowers from Walmart. Gary had desired a fancy ceremony, but she'd nixed the idea. She'd wanted it over and done with the least amount of fanfare. Maybe that was why she'd been so determined to make Ginger's wedding a special affair.

"I still can't believe Ginger's getting married," Matt murmured, standing so close to Savannah she could smell the heady scent of his cologne.

"Yes," Savannah agreed, emotions choking her throat. "My little sister's all grown up."

"Weddings are kind of sad, aren't they?"

His sensitivity surprised her. Had he sensed the mixed feelings stirring inside her? She wanted happiness for Ginger, but at the same time, she would miss her sister something fierce.

She glanced at him. "They can bring back sad memories, yes."

He rested a hand on her shoulder, his touch sending tremors of longing contracting through her muscles. "You know, Savvy, I'd always thought we'd get married someday. Funny how things work out."

She closed her eyes, clenched her jaw. Why did he have to say that? She carried enough regret in her heart to last a lifetime. Maybe she'd made a mistake when she married Gary, but there was nothing she could do about it now.

Stepping away from his dangerous touch, Savannah opened her eyes and turned to face him. "Have you found my cattle yet?"

The corner of his left eye twitched, and he pressed his lips into a firm, straight line, a sure sign her question upset him. "A few head turned up at an auction in Midland," he said tersely. "Their brands had been altered."

"They're my cattle?"

He nodded.

"That's great. How many?"

"Six."

"Where are they?"

His brown eyes darkened. "Still in Midland."

"How come? Why haven't you brought them home?" She settled her hands on her hips. Savannah knew he was hiding something. Matt had never been good at keeping secrets from her.

Dropping his gaze, he shifted his weight. "They're being held as evidence. The cattle are impounded until the investigation is over."

She frowned and rubbed her brow with her index finger and thumb. "I'm afraid I don't understand."

"Do you have more tables to move?" he asked.

His evasiveness served to pique her curiosity. What was

going on? "Is that your way of saying you can't talk about the investigation?"

He looked relieved. "Yeah."

"Fine." She shrugged. "Let's finish moving the tables."

Neither spoke as they worked. One minute he'd been open with her, the next elusive. Two years ago, she could have coaxed him to talk, but now? No way. She knew he wouldn't confide in her, and honestly, she couldn't blame him. She'd violated his trust. If only they could erase the past and start over with a clean slate.

Wishful thinking, Savannah.

"Need me for anything else?" Matt raised an eyebrow when they were done moving tables.

"Not right now. I've got to give Cody his lunch."

Matt inclined his head toward the barn. "I think I'll go have a talk with your ranch hand."

"Clem? What for?"

"I'd like to question him again about the night of the thefts, make sure he didn't forget something."

"Okay." She was glad for any excuse to escape.

Matt stalked to the barn, and Savannah went inside the house. She blew her breath out through puffed cheeks. Would she survive this day?

Ginger sat at the kitchen table polishing her fingernails. She gave Savannah a weak smile. "Cody's napping," she said, "I fed him, and Aunt Pearl just called. She and Cousin Ada are in Rascal. They'll be here in a few minutes."

"Oh, boy. I'd hoped the guests wouldn't start arriving so soon." Savannah pushed her bangs from her forehead and sat down beside Ginger.

"Vannah, I'm getting nervous."

Savannah patted her sister's shoulder. "You'll be fine, honey."

"But I hate getting up in front of people, and we've got a hundred guests coming."

"It's not the same thing as giving a speech, and besides, Todd will be right beside you."

"Did you have second thoughts when you got married?"

And thirds and fourths and fifths. Savannah wished Ginger would stop trying to compare their weddings. It wasn't the same thing at all. Ginger was in love with Todd.

"Honey, you've just got the jitters. Everything will be all right."

"Where's Matt?"

"Outside talking to Clem. Why?"

Ginger wiggled her pearly pink fingernails. "Would you be offended if I asked him to give me away?"

"I... I thought you wanted me to give you away."

"Well, you have been both mother and father to me, and I love you with all my heart, but I'd feel more proper if a man gave me away, and since we don't have any close male family members..." Ginger looked at Savannah, a pleading expression on her face. "I mean," Ginger amended quickly, "if you'd rather I didn't ask him, I won't. I know there are bad feelings between you two, and the last thing I want to do is hurt your feelings."

"Sure, honey." Savannah smiled gamely. "Go ahead and ask Matt, if that's what you really want."

"Ask me what?" Matt opened the screen door and stepped into the kitchen.

Ginger and Savannah looked at each other. Savannah lifted her shoulders.

"I was wondering," Ginger began, springing up from her chair like a jack-in-the-box. "If you would consider giving me away."

"Uh..." Matt looked flabbergasted.

"Don't feel obligated to say yes," Ginger said. "It's just

that I've always thought of you as a big brother, and since I don't have a father or brothers of my own..." She trailed off.

"Why I'd be honored, Ginger, but I'm not exactly dressed for the occasion." He indicated his attire with a sweep of his hand.

"You look great," Ginger said. "Just like the Matt Forrester I used to know and love. I wouldn't recognize you in a suit."

"Savvy?" Matt looked at her.

"It's Ginger's wedding," Savannah said. "It's up to her."

8

Matt shot an uneasy glance in Savannah's direction. He'd come here today prepared to take Savannah down to the sheriff's department for questioning, not give her sister away on her wedding day.

"Who was supposed to give you away?"

"Vannah."

"You don't mind?" Matt asked Savannah.

Savannah held her arms open wide. "Please, be my guest. One less thing I've got to worry about."

"You could be my matron of honor instead," Ginger said.

Savannah shook her head. "No, your best friend, Karen, would be so disappointed. I'll be all right."

"But I want you to be in the wedding, sis," Ginger insisted.

"Really, Ginger, it's okay. I'll sit in the front row with Cody and act as the mother of the bride."

"I don't want to come between the two of you," Matt interrupted. "Savannah can still give you away."

"Matt, nothing would please me more than for Ginger to come down the aisle on your arm. Both of you, it's all right."

"Well, if you're sure... But I'm going to run home and get a suit to wear. I want to do this up right," Matt said.

"Oh, thanks," Ginger exclaimed, hugging Matt with her palms held out so that she wouldn't muss up her freshly painted fingernails. "You're special."

And an idiot, he thought.

Why did he persist in getting personally involved with Savannah? Hooking up with her again was flat out stupid, especially if she was involved in the disappearance of the livestock.

"Thank you," Savannah said, gratitude on her face.

Cody awoke and started squalling from the bedroom at the same time Savannah's relatives arrived on the front porch.

Time passed in a blur as Matt found himself reintroduced to people he'd met briefly years before. The ensuing hubbub provided a decent cover while he dashed home for a change of clothes.

When he returned, Matt pitched in where he was needed —running errands, toting parcels, directing traffic. The whole time he worked, he couldn't forget the reason he'd come to the Circle B and the ugly task that awaited him as soon as the wedding ceremony was over.

If the suspect had been anyone other than his ex-girlfriend, he would have taken them in right away, but his affection for Savannah prevented him from doing so. He recognized his weakness, acknowledged it with shame. A good lawman didn't show favoritism.

Face it, Forrester. You're between a rock and a hard place.

How could he drag Savannah away from her sister's wedding, particularly when he'd been invited to give the bride away?

By the time four o'clock rolled around, Savannah was a basket case. What with getting herself and Cody dressed, offering moral support to Ginger, and herding a houseful of relatives and taffeta-draped bridesmaids, she desperately needed to stop and take several deep breaths. Yet somehow, she'd managed to pull the whole thing off.

She found herself sitting in the front row under the white awning, Cody clutched in her lap, friends, and family seated around her.

Although she was reluctant to admit it, Matt had been a big help. He'd joked with Ginger, charmed her relatives, doled out words of manly wisdom to a pale-faced Todd. He'd acted as a gofer, a butler, and even stepped in to usher guests to their seats. He was indispensable.

The weather cooperated, issuing a slight breeze and plenty of sunshine. The fragrant odor of flowers hung in the air—honeysuckle mingled with roses, orchids complemented daisies, snapdragons enhanced marigolds. The garden was beautiful in shades of red, purple, blue, yellow, and pink. Nature heralded the festive, happy occasion in exotic splashes of color and intoxicating smells.

The guests dressed accordingly. The women were decked out in bright, cheerful finery. The men sported suits or Texas tuxedoes, the children clad in patent leather and ribbons.

Over to one side, the caterers stood by the tables, ready to set up for the reception once the ceremony ended. Todd's family sat in the aisle across from Savannah. They smiled, nodding their heads in greeting. She swallowed a lump in her throat, sorry that her mother hadn't lived to share this joyous day with her daughters.

She clutched Cody tighter.

Lilting music rose and fell as the guitarist strummed a soulful tune of love and sacrifice. The minister assumed his position at the front of the altar. The crowd rustled. Heads turned as the bridesmaids started down the walkway, delicate as mauve swans.

Todd and his best man were in place. And as the strains of the wedding march began, Savannah's palms grew cold and sweaty with anticipation.

Earlier they had decided Ginger and Matt would enter from around the side of the house and walk down a path of green carpeting rolled out for the occasion. Savannah's hands trembled, and she clasped them firmly around Cody's to gain control. She rose to her feet, the congregation following her lead.

She caught her breath as Matt and Ginger stepped into sight.

Her sister looked so beautiful.

And Matt...handsome didn't begin to describe him. He wore a gray three-piece suit and a crisp white shirt. A smart red tie was knotted at his throat. With his dark hair combed off his forehead and the sunlight dappling over his face, he was utterly gorgeous. He'd gone beyond the call of duty by agreeing to walk Ginger down the aisle. The generous gesture reminded Savannah of why she'd fallen in love with him in the first place.

Ginger and Matt moved forward, and Savannah couldn't take her eyes off him. Her sister's elbow crooked through his, her bouquet grasped to her chest.

Pride swelled inside Savannah. She'd vowed she wouldn't cry, but that had been a stupid promise. Tears ran down her cheeks as she watched her sister head for the altar on the arm of the man who should have been *her* husband.

This is how her wedding should have been—full of hope and promise. The joining of two people who truly loved one another embarking on life's greatest adventure together instead of a sad, brittle marriage of convenience. She should have married Matt instead of Gary. But cancer had had other plans.

Savannah caught Matt's eye. He seemed to read her mind. An expression of pure longing crossed his face. That yearning look gave her hope. She'd made so many errors. Was it too late to undo them?

The music reached a crescendo at the same time Matt and Ginger arrived in front of the minister. The preacher raised his hand, and the music stopped.

"Friends! Family! Welcome!" the man began enthusiastically. "We have gathered here today to witness the union of these two young people in holy matrimony."

His words blurred as he continued the ritual. Savannah didn't hear him. She focused on Matt and Ginger, her pulse thumping so hard and fast she feared she might faint.

Cody squirmed, and she absentmindedly patted his back.

"Who gives this woman to be wed?" the preacher called out, glancing directly at Matt.

"Her sister and me," Matt said, his voice rumbling so deep and resonant, it created a quiver in Savannah's stomach.

Her sister and me.

As if she and Matt were together.

Matt stepped back to join Savannah on the front row.

"She's breathtaking," he whispered.

"Thank you for giving her away," Savannah whispered back. "It was definitely above the call of duty."

They stared forward, every eye on Todd and Ginger as the minister led the couple through their vows.

Cody tugged at Savannah's hair, and she shifted him into her left arm. Before she knew what was happening, Matt reached over, grasped Savannah's right hand, and squeezed it.

His touch suffused her with warmth. His nearness sent her emotions spinning out of control. His fingers twining with hers had her pulse skittering a frantic beat. Goodness gracious, was she falling in love with him all over again?

The thought terrified her. She twisted her hand away just as the couple pledged their troth.

From the corner of her eye, she saw Matt's jaw stiffen.

The minister pronounced Todd and Ginger husband and wife. After a memorable kiss, the newlyweds turned and started down the carpeted path, followed by their attendants. The guests watched them disappear into the house, then they dispersed about the lawn to wait for the reception.

Anxious to distance herself from Matt, Savannah allowed Aunt Pearl to hold Cody while she went to oversee the buffet setup. Matt positioned himself out of the way, his arms crossed over his chest, his eagle-eyed gaze missing nothing.

Various friends and relatives came up to Savannah to offer their congratulations, and she used the opportunity to ignore him.

Ginger and Todd returned to the gathering, flushed and beaming. Savannah suspected they'd exchanged some heavy-duty kissing while in the house. A trace of lipstick clung to Todd's collar, and her sister's hair was attractively mussed.

They formed a receiving line, and to Savannah's dismay, Ginger tugged Matt over to join them. Sandwiched between Matt and her sister, Savannah plastered a smile on her face and endured.

"I'm not enjoying this any more than you are," Matt mumbled out of the corner of his mouth.

"What do you mean? I'm thrilled," she growled, low and gruff so only he could hear.

"Liar."

"Why did you come here today?" she asked through clenched teeth, forcing a smile as she shook a guest's hand.

He slid a sideways glance in her direction, then nodded at the row of people extending their hands in congratulation.

"Soon as these folks leave, Savannah, you and I are going to have a serious discussion."

His reply and the look on his face alarmed her.

"So you *did* come for some other reason besides Ginger's wedding. I knew it." Savannah's facial muscles ached from smiling. "Hello, Mr. and Mrs. Branch, glad you could make it."

Hiram and Myra Branch, whose nearby ranch, The Triple Fork, specialized in training thoroughbred race-horses, responded kindly but Savannah barely heard a word. She kept thinking about what Matt had said. What did he want to speak to her about? The sun beat down, suddenly no longer merely warm, but uncomfortably hot.

Thankfully, the procession of well-wishers ended, and everyone dispersed to enjoy the refreshments. The photographer called for the wedding party to assemble themselves while the guitarist broke into a lively tune. Whimsical chords filled the garden.

"Come on, folks, gather round," the photographer said. "You too, sis," he called to Savannah. "Don't go running off, I'm sure Ginger wants you in the pictures as well."

Savannah went over.

"Let's get your husband over here, too." The cameraman waved at Matt.

"He's not my husband."

"Can Matt be in the picture anyway, Vannah?" Ginger asked.

Savannah sighed. She could refuse her sister nothing today, and Ginger knew it. "Sure. Why not?"

Matt joined them. The wedding party stood in the broiling sun, following the photographer's instructions—changing position, posing, pasting smiles on their faces. First Matt's arm across Savannah's shoulder, then around her waist, finally him holding her hand. Savannah gritted her teeth and endured.

Thirty minutes later, the photographer clapped his hands. "Okay, everyone, that's a wrap."

Savannah searched the crowd for Aunt Pearl, eager to retrieve Cody and distance herself from Matt.

"Why he's the most precious angel," Aunt Pearl cooed as she relinquished Cody. "But I must be getting old. Holding him for so long has worn me to a frazzle."

"Thanks for watching him, Auntie. Why don't you go get some cake and punch and sit down? I'll come visit with you in a sec. I think Cody needs changing."

Aunt Pearl fumbled in her pocket for a blue tissue and pressed it to her eyes. "Your mama would have been so proud. It was a lovely wedding, Savannah. You outdid yourself."

She patted her elderly great-aunt's shoulder. "That's nice of you to say so." Head down, she scurried through the throng and finally made it to the house.

"Let me get the door for you."

Matt stepped from nowhere to open the screen. Damn him. Why couldn't he simply go away and leave her alone?

Without another word, he followed her through the house and into Cody's bedroom. Savannah flicked on the light, settled her son in his crib, and grabbed a fresh diaper.

Matt leaned against the wall, his long legs stretched out in front of him, his arms folded across his chest. "Savvy, we've got to talk."

Her hands trembled slightly as she eased the wet diaper off Cody and wiped his bottom with a moist towelette. She cleared her throat. "What about?"

"That Santa Gertrudis herd."

Her stomach fluttered ominously. He seemed so serious.

"So talk," she said lightly.

"Not here," he replied.

"Where?"

He moved across the room, reached out, and took her elbow. Spinning her around, he forced her to look him in the eyes. "I'm sorry to do this to you, Savannah, but I have to take you back to the sheriff's department for questioning."

SAVANNAH BLINKED. HAD SHE HEARD CORRECTLY? SHE WAS a suspect?

Cody gurgled, pulling her attention away from Matt and back to her son.

"Did you hear me, Savvy?" he asked.

"I have to diaper Cody," she mumbled, her mind whirling with the implications of Matt's statement.

"You have to go to the sheriff's department with me."

She bit her bottom lip. "Am ... I under arrest?"

"No," he said. "Not yet."

"But... what did I do?"

"We need an official statement from you, but I can't discuss the details here. Please. Let's just see your guests off, and then we'll leave."

"That's why you came here in the first place, wasn't it? To arrest me?"

Matt sighed, threading his fingers through his hair. "I came to take you in for questioning, not to arrest you."

She fastened the diaper securely around Cody's body. What had she done wrong? Confusion clouded her mind, and she couldn't think straight.

"I'd forgotten it was Ginger's wedding day," he mumbled.

"Well, thank you for waiting until the wedding was over. It would have ruined everything for Ginger if you'd interrupted the ceremony."

"I know."

"We don't have to tell her about this, do we?"

Matt shook his head. She picked Cody up and held him to her shoulder. Matt stuffed his hands into his suit pockets. He appeared weary, exhausted, A five o'clock shadow shaded his jaw, and a worried furrow creased his brow.

"Okay," she said quietly.

Because she felt confident the whole matter would be straightened out in a few minutes, she refused to get upset. No cause for panic. She'd done nothing wrong.

They joined the group outside for the reception. Three hours later, Todd and Ginger left for their honeymoon trip to Cancun while the guests slowly filtered away. By nine p.m. only Matt, Savannah, Clem, Cody, and the caterers remained.

"You ready?" Matt asked, dangling the Jeep keys from his index finger.

Her satin dress was crumpled. Her new high-heeled shoes bit her toes. She wanted to ask him if she could change, but he'd been kind enough to postpone this ordeal until after the wedding. She didn't feel right asking for more favors.

"What am I going to do with Cody?" she asked fretfully, pushing back a lock of hair that had fallen from her elaborate hairdo.

"Bring him along. I'll watch him during the questioning."

"You won't be conducting the interrogation?"

"No," Matt said.

And Savannah couldn't decide if that made things better or worse.

9

Matt heard the anxious keen in her voice, and the sound burned his gut. "I can't conduct the interview. I'm not impartial. And it's not an interrogation, Savvy. Just a few questions."

"Are you sure, Matt?"

What could he tell her? That by the end of the night she might possibly find herself locked in a jail cell? Matt shuddered at the image. He simply could not believe she was guilty of deliberate fraud, but he wouldn't be doing his job if he didn't take her in.

The trip into Rascal was a solemn one.

The final rays of dying spring sunlight slanted in through Matt's window. He snatched occasional sidelong glimpses of Savannah as they drove. Her pale ivory skin glowed like a beacon. Her full, lush lips turned down in a sad expression.

The sight snagged strings of loneliness deep in Matt's soul. How he wanted to draw her into his arms and comfort her, to kiss her and tell her not to worry. But he couldn't. He'd already gone too far allowing his emotions to affect his judgment.

He called in and told Midge, the dispatcher, he was bringing Savannah to the department. The radio crackled, and Sheriff Langley's voice came on the line. "'Bout time, son. I was fixing to put out an APB on the both of you. Thought you'd gotten lost."

"Did I get you into trouble?" Savannah asked after the sheriff signed off.

"Naw." He shrugged.

"Thanks again for waiting." She stared down at the floorboard.

Lord, he felt like such a jerk. Sometimes his job was the pits.

They pulled into the parking lot of the sheriff's department. Matt killed the engine, then got out and helped Savannah and Cody out.

Holding the toddler on one hip, he took Savannah's elbow and escorted her inside the building.

"Hey, Joe," he greeted a young officer lounging back in his chair at the front desk. "Why don't you get your feet off the desk?"

Joe dropped his feet to the floor, sat up straight, glanced from Matt to the baby to Savannah and back again, then hid a snicker behind his hand. "You look plumb fatherly, Forrester."

"Something wrong with that?" Matt asked dryly.

"No, sir."

"Then you won't mind keeping your comments to yourself."

"Sheriff Langley's been grumbling about you all afternoon," Joe said.

"Yeah? Where is he?"

"Right here." Sheriff Patrick Langley loomed in the doorway of the jail.

"What are you doing here so late on a Saturday evening?" Matt asked his boss.

Sheriff Langley grimaced. "Mae's out of town visiting her sister and to tell you the truth, the house is pretty lonesome without her."

"Couldn't you find a better place to hang out?" Matt asked.

"You're one to talk, Forrester. You work more hours than I do."

It was true. He readily confessed to his workaholic nature. No one waited for him in his empty apartment.

The sheriff smiled. "You must be Savannah."

"Yes, sir," she replied.

Pat Langley stepped forward, extending his hand. "I knew your husband, Gary. Fine man. Sorry to hear about his passing."

"Thank you."

"And I'm really sorry to disturb you, ma'am, especially at this late hour." He shot Matt an accusing glance.

"Am I under arrest for something?" Savannah asked in a quiet, subdued voice that made Matt ache.

Her slender shoulders slumped in defeat, and the material of her satiny dress whispered as she moved. He wanted to gather her close and erase her concerns and problems. There was no way he could be the one to question her. He'd totally lost all objectivity.

"Oh, no, ma'am. We've just got to get a few things straight about your missing cattle. Things just aren't adding up."

"I see." She twisted her fingers together.

"Let's go into my office and have an informal chat. Would you like a cup of coffee? Or something else to drink?"

"What about Cody?"

"Forrester can look after him."

Matt nodded. "Sure."

"He hasn't had his supper yet." Savannah nibbled her bottom lip.

"Don't worry," Matt insisted. "I'll find something for him to eat."

Laying a hand on Savannah's shoulder, Sheriff Langley guided her toward his office. She looked at Matt, fear in her eyes.

Damn. Damn. Damn. Matt spun on his heels, unable to bear her despair.

He hated this part of the job. When innocent people suddenly found themselves afoul of the law. What he liked was chasing the bad guys and seeing them get their just desserts, but this? Walking as swiftly as his legs would take him, Matt left the building for the fresh, clean night air, Cody riding comfortably at his hip. The boy's fuzzy halo of hair stirred in the breeze.

"Da?" he asked, placing a tiny finger on Matt's chin.

"No, I'm not your Da." Matt whispered. "But I sure as hell wish I were."

It was true, he realized. For a man whose job had always been everything, he now wanted a wife and kids. And not just any wife and kids. He wanted Savannah. He wanted Cody. When had his thinking changed?

Cody's face wrinkled. He whimpered.

"Now, now, little fella, don't go changing your moods on me that quick." Matt held him in both hands and jostled him gently.

A sad, worried expression crinkled Cody's eyes. His bottom lip quivered. Did the kid sense something was wrong?

"Come on, none of that." Matt tucked him in the crook of one arm and started across the parking lot. Before he reached the Jeep, Cody exploded into a full-fledged howl.

Gritting his teeth, Matt settled the baby in his car seat. Huge crocodile tears rolled down the child's cheeks. Oh, Lord. What had he gotten himself into?

Get a grip, Forrester. If you can wrangle thieves and murderers, you can definitely handle one tiny kid.

Cody's squalling increased.

"Okay, okay. Food."

What in Sam Hill did babies eat? He certainly hoped Savannah wasn't still breastfeeding the little tyke.

"Want a hamburger?"

Cody hiccupped.

"Does that sound good?"

The kid stared at him and sniffled.

"Right. Bad idea." He needed something baby food-ish. Mashed potatoes or a banana. He could stop by the store, then take Cody back to his apartment to feed him.

Matt found a Stop & Shop. Cody's sobs dwindled to soft sighs. Matt undid the boy from his car seat. Lifting the boy onto his shoulders for a piggyback ride, Matt clamped his palms across those chubby little thighs. Instantly, tears turned to giggles as Cody clutched Matt's hair in both hands. Matt grinned. Did he possess a natural gift with babies or what?

"Okay, kiddo, what'll it be?" He stood before a shelf of baby food and surveyed the selection. "Strained peas?" Matt made a face. "Carrots? Green beans? Apricots?"

"Da!"

"Yeah, that's what you always say. We're going to have to do some serious work on your vocabulary, son."

Son.

Why had he said that word? Wishful thinking?

The front door of the opened and two men slunk in. Matt noticed their scruffy reflection in the security mirror, but because he'd been fixated on finding supper for Cody, his sixth sense didn't kick in immediately. As it was, by the time the hairs on the back of his neck prickled a warning, the men had yanked ski masks over their faces and drawn pistols on the store clerk.

"Open the cash register. Give us the money. Now!" the taller of the two men growled.

Oh, hell. Matt swung Cody from his shoulders into the crook of his arm in one fluid motion. Crouching to the ground, he prayed the men hadn't noticed him.

Instinct had him reaching for the 9mm Walther he wore in a shoulder holster. His hand patted his unadorned chest. His duty weapon wasn't there. He'd removed it for Ginger's wedding and had neglected to strap it back on when the wedding was over. Just as well. Best not have any gunplay with a baby in his arms.

Cody whimpered.

Hush, kid, not now.

The baby stared at him wide-eyed.

Matt had never dodged a fight in his life. But what could he do?

He heard the jangle of coins hitting the floor and tasted the bile of his own frustration rising in his throat. He should be able to stop this robbery. Instead, Cody rendered him useless. Matt stared at the row of breakfast cereal in front of his face.

Every muscle in his body corded, every nerve ending zinged on full alert. He duckwalked forward, Cody still clutched in his arm.

"Hurry! Hurry!" one of the robbers barked. Matt listened closely to the voice, memorizing it for future reference.

The slap of running feet and the sound of the door being slammed open.

Matt popped to a standing position, Cody cradled next to his side like a football in a running back's arms. He took off after the robbers, ignoring the startled, whey-faced clerk standing behind the counter with his hands still raised over his head.

The two suspects leaped into a dented black Camaro and

blasted out of the parking lot. Matt opened the door to his Jeep and fastened Cody into the car seat as quickly as possible, his gaze trained on the disappearing vehicle.

By the time he got behind the wheel and roared after them, they had careened around a corner, narrowly avoiding an accident with oncoming traffic. Matt slapped the portable siren to the roof, stomped on the accelerator, and shot after the robbers.

❧

"Now, Savannah. I don't want you to feel nervous. That's why I brought you to my office instead of the interrogation room. That place can be pretty intimidating." Sheriff Langley smiled at her, yet she felt anything but reassured.

"I'm not intimidated," she fibbed.

"Have a seat." He waved at a hard-backed wooden chair with his hand.

She perched on the edge of the chair and took a deep breath. "I don't understand why I'm here."

Anxiety knotted her stomach. The police band radio in the corner crackled and hissed. She stared at the jovial-faced man across from her. He looked like a dark-haired Santa Claus instead of a lawman. She worried her bottom lip with her teeth. The room was too warm. Perspiration pooled in the hollow space at the base of her neck. She felt slightly nauseous.

"We've determined that the theft of your cattle is not related to the other robberies Detective Forrester's been investigating."

"Meaning?"

"Nothing, in and of itself." He shifted in his chair, laced his fingers together, and laid them over his expansive belly.

She waited.

"What concerns me, Mrs. Markum is the fact that your husband took out a large insurance policy on that Santa Gertrudis herd before he died. A policy drawn up by your new brother-in-law, and that is due to lapse by the end of this month if the premium isn't paid."

Savannah gasped and raised a hand to her throat. The news rocked her. "What? Are you sure? Todd never told me about any insurance policy on the cattle."

Sheriff Langley pushed a copy of the policy across the desk toward her. "Are you telling me you didn't know anything about it?"

"Absolutely not. Where did you get this?" She picked up the papers and scanned them. She recognized Gary's distinctive scrawl at the bottom of the page.

The sheriff pursed his lips in a pensive expression. "Detective Forrester found it in the paperwork you gave him."

"Let me get this straight. You suspect me of insurance fraud even when I never made a claim on the policy?"

"We have to weigh all the evidence. You're in debt to the teeth. For all I know, you and Gary planned this together so you could save the ranch after his death."

"That's ridiculous."

Sheriff Langley cocked a skeptical eyebrow. "Sounds plausible to me."

"Why would I be stupid enough to give the insurance papers to Matt if I were involved in such a scheme?" Did the man believe she was a complete idiot?

The sheriff shrugged. "You and Detective Forrester were almost engaged once. Perhaps you hoped to cut him in on the deal."

Savannah jumped to her feet, clasping her arms to her chest. "I don't believe this."

"Simmer down. I want you to see this from my point of view."

She tossed her head. "Even if I were trying to pull off insurance fraud, I definitely would not take on Matt Forrester as a partner. He lives and breathes his job. I know. I was his girlfriend. He'd never do anything to jeopardize his livelihood."

Sheriff Langley scratched his head. "Well, I'm glad to hear you say so. Why don't you sit back down?"

Reluctantly, Savannah sank onto the chair once more.

"Let's start from the top. You tell me everything that happened the day you discovered the herd missing."

In minute detail, Savannah relayed the events of the day that intersected her path with Matt's once again. When she finished, the sheriff frowned, leaned back in his chair, and stuck his thumbs through his belt loops.

"Anybody else know about this insurance policy?" he asked.

Savannah lifted her shoulders. "*I* didn't even know about it."

"Think. Any relatives of your husband's? Friends? Your ranch hand?"

"No." Savannah shook her head. "Gary had a few friends, but they haven't been around much since he passed on. Although he does have a half-brother in prison. I know you remember Connor Heller and all the mess that happened Christmas before last at Wren and Keegan's dairy."

The sheriff nodded. "Most excitement we've had in Rascal in years, not counting Kurt McNally getting engaged to that Hollywood actress, Elizabeth Destiny. But Heller is in maximum security in Huntsville. He's not in on this."

"You sure?"

"What about Clement Olson?"

"Clem?" Savannah gave a short laugh. "He's worked at the Circle B for twenty years. I trust him completely."

"Hmph," the sheriff grunted.

"I suppose I'm still your number one suspect."

"There is one thing in your favor."

"Yes?"

"You didn't try to make a claim on the policy."

Good thing she hadn't known about it. She would have paid off some debts, hired more hands, and gotten the ranch back on its feet. She admired Gary for his foresight. He had no idea the insurance policy would land her in this trouble.

The radio squawked. A garbled message came through. Sheriff Langley leaned over and fiddled with the dials.

"Midge..." A voice faded in and out.

"Dang thing." Sheriff Langley slapped the offending equipment. "We need a new one, but the county won't approve the expenditure."

The static cleared. "This is Forrester." His voice came through tinny and far away.

Savannah sat up straight, instantly at attention.

The sheriff grabbed the receiver. "I'll intercept the signal, Midge," he hollered at the dispatcher over the intercom. "Go ahead, Matt, what's up?"

"Sheriff, I'm in pursuit of a 1998 black Camaro, license number GWS-675, southbound on Presidio Boulevard."

Savannah jumped up again. "What! What did he say?"

Matt had been watching Cody, and now he was in hot pursuit of a speeding vehicle? Was Cody still with him? What had happened? Where was her son? Terror seized her.

Sheriff Langley frowned, waving Savannah into silence. "What's the offense, Forrester?"

"The perps just robbed the Stop & Shop on Broadway. I was an eyewitness."

Her heart pounded in hideous slow motion. She had

instant visions of a fiery car crash—twisted fenders, mangled metal, the lifeless body of her toddler son thrown from the wreckage.

"Oh God," Savannah shrieked, no longer able to contain herself. "Tell him to stop right now. He's got our baby in the car with him!"

10

What was he doing? Matt squeezed the radio's receiver in his hand and looked over at Cody.

Something inexplicable happened.

For once, something took precedence over making a bust. All his adult life, he'd put service to his job as the number one priority in his life. Nothing else had ever come before duty. Not his folks. Not his friends. Not even Savannah. But this sleepy-eyed baby with the fuzzy halo of hair caught him up short.

Had he lost his ever loving mind? Chasing after armed criminals at high speeds with an infant in the car?

In his moment of hesitation, the Camaro sprinted farther away.

"Forrester!" Patrick Langley's voice resonated over the speaker. "Are you still there?"

Up ahead a stoplight turned from yellow to red, and Matt knew he would not run it. He gently braked to a stop as the Camaro disappeared from view. He spoke gruffly into the receiver. "Yeah, boss, I'm still here."

"You got a baby with you?"

Matt briefly closed his eyes, swallowing hard. "Yep. He's here with me."

"Is he all right?" Matt heard Savannah's high-pitched voice in the background, bordering on hysteria.

"I've stopped the pursuit, sir."

"Good," the sheriff barked. "Get your rear end back here, pronto."

"On my way," he replied and cradled the radio.

By the time he returned to the office, Cody had fallen asleep. Rather than risk waking the baby, he took him out of the Jeep, car seat and all. The minute he walked through the door, he saw Savannah pacing the hallway, the high-heeled shoes she'd worn at Ginger's wedding striking a sharp staccato on the concrete floor. Hands cocked on her hips, her eyes flashing pure liquid fire, she was an irate mother, more dangerous than a truckload of felons.

Midge, Joe, and Sheriff Langley arranged themselves around the front desk, poised as if waiting for the second act of an exciting new play and a bucket of hot buttered popcorn.

"Matthew Cody Forrester," Savannah said, her tone low but deadly. "What in the world were you thinking taking a baby on a high-speed car chase?"

He hadn't seen her this mad since...well, he'd never seen her this mad. Guilt gnawed at his craw. He couldn't fault her rage. He had overstepped the bounds of rational behavior. She was right.

And damn, if she didn't look fine.

Despite the wrinkles creased into her sapphire dress, she sparkled like Cinderella before the stroke of midnight. Her hair curled in honey-brown rings around her delicate earlobes. Her skin glowed, pretty as sun-ripened peaches. The black velvet ribbon secured at her long, slender throat completed the enchanting package. How had he survived two years without her in his life?

Arousal, hard and fast, ambushed him like a bolt of lightning on a cloudless afternoon. How he wanted her! To kiss her, caress her, and drive himself into her soft, willing body and allow her sweetness to envelope him in a frenzy of animal passion.

Transfixed, Matt stared, unable to speak.

Savannah stalked toward him, her hands outstretched. "Give him to me."

Adrenaline from the car chase mixed inside him with spurts of testosterone until he felt as jittery as if he'd downed a hundred cups of Sheriff Langley's wicked black coffee.

She snatched the car seat from him. Cody opened his eyes during the ensuing jostle, blinked at his mother, and burst into tears.

"See what you did!"

"Me? You're the one who jerked him around."

If looks could kill, Matt would have been charred toast. Holding the car seat against a raised knee, she struggled to snap Cody free from the restraining contraption.

"Let me help," Matt offered.

"I don't need your help," she barked.

Cody howled louder.

To keep from agitating her more, Matt took a step backward.

Midge, Joe, and Sheriff Langley ducked their heads to hide grins. Matt scowled in their general direction.

Finally, Savannah released Cody and allowed the car seat to slide to the floor while she raised him to her shoulder.

"Is it too much to hope that maybe you fed him before you placed his life in jeopardy?"

"That's what I was attempting to do before we got interrupted by a holdup in progress. Excuse me for being in the wrong place at the wrong time."

"Bull. You love being in the middle of a fight."

"That's not fair," he protested.

She was on a roll, shaking a pearly pink fingernail in his face. "You didn't have to play the hero, but you did. Always the lawman even when you're off duty. You don't even care that Cody could have been killed. You can't control yourself. You have to be a macho male. It's a sickness."

"If I hadn't been controlling myself, *Mrs. Markum,* I would have returned with the suspects in question." He pivoted on his boot heel and slanted the sheriff a sideways glance. "Did you send the Rascal Leos after the perps?" he asked, referring to the town's small police force.

"Of course. But I know it hurts for you to let the perps go," Sheriff Langley said.

"You shouldn't have followed them as far as you did." Savannah glowered.

"Dang it, Savvy." Matt ran a hand through his hair. "I stopped, okay? What more do you want from me? A pint of blood? Cody's safe. No harm done."

"And you wonder why I didn't marry you," she said, her tone cold enough to cause frostbite.

The resulting silence echoed in the hallway. Savannah stared at him.

Matt knew he'd screwed up and immediately felt contrite. She was just worried about her child.

"I'm sorry," he mumbled.

Her chin quivered. She turned to Sheriff Langley. "I want to go home now."

Matt moved toward her and held out his hand. Sidestepping, she kept a firm hand pressed to Cody's back.

"I'll take you home," he insisted.

"I rather someone else take me home."

That hurt, but she was upset. He understood why she didn't want to be around him right now.

Sheriff Langley interceded. He placed a big paw on Matt's

shoulder and tugged him backward. "Come on, Matt, let's go in my office and have a talk. Joe will take Savannah home."

❧

THE GRANDFATHER CLOCK IN THE LIVING ROOM WAS striking midnight by the time Savannah finished feeding Cody and rocked him to sleep. After the twelfth echoing bong, the house fell silent in the looming emptiness.

The rocker creaked as Savannah shifted, the weight of Cody's head resting on her arm. Sounds of chirping crickets filtered in through the open window, wafting on the pleasant breeze that ruffled the white lace curtains.

The place felt so lonely without Ginger. Already she missed her sister more than she'd ever missed her husband. Ashamed at her disloyal thoughts, Savannah placed a gentle kiss on Cody's nose. If it hadn't been for Gary, she didn't know what would have happened to her and Ginger after their mother's death.

Matt would have taken care of you if you'd given him a chance.

Memories assailed her in a backlash of emotion. Matt—defending her virtue against unwanted advances from a local ruffian. Matt—romancing her at the lake, complete with a candlelight dinner and flowers. Matt—taking her for a ride on his stallion. Matt—risking his life to break up a bar fight.

An unexpected tear trailed down her face. She didn't wipe it away, instead allowed it to roll off her chin and plop onto the soft material of her pink cotton sleep shirt. She mourned her past, her losses, her mistakes. She wished desperately she could turn back the clock and do things differently. She wished her mother were alive to comfort her. In the end, all the wishing in the world was fruitless.

The sheriff suspected her of insurance fraud. Her ranch was operating in the red and slipping deeper into debt. She was alone on the place with just a baby and an old man for company, both of whom depended on her.

And then there was Matt.

Things were so complicated, but she had to tell him that Cody was his son, even if it meant breaking her promise to Gary. How did she go about dropping *that* bombshell? He was going to be angry, and so hurt.

Biting her bottom lip, Savannah closed her eyes. There was no way she could make it up to him.

Cody stirred, stuck his thumb in his mouth, and sucked.

Savannah sighed. Her whole body ached with exhaustion, but her mind whirled. She had to be up at dawn to help Clem feed the livestock, and with Ginger gone, there was no one to help with Cody.

Forcing herself to move, she got to her feet and headed for the bedroom. Instead of putting Cody in his crib, she nestled him next to her in the big, fluffy bed and tucked the covers securely around them. Taking a deep breath, she rested her head on her hands and stared at the ceiling, willing her thoughts to quiet.

Her motives in breaking up with Matt had been pure, but one question kept circling her brain. Could Matt ever forgive her for keeping him from his son?

MATT HAD A PEACE OFFERING.

In the back of the rented trailer hitched to his Jeep were six Santa Gertrudis cows, swaying and mooing. After talking half the night, he'd finally convinced Sheriff Langley to let him return the cattle to Savannah. They'd both agreed she was not involved in the theft.

That made him feel better. He hated being suspicious of

her, but his job required him to accept nothing at face value, not even the woman he had once loved so hopelessly.

And he longed to slip back into Savannah's good graces. He had to make amends for his behavior last night when he'd exercised the poorest judgment of his career and lit out after those robbers with her child in his car. He hadn't thought. Just reacted.

Matt slammed the trailer gate shut, thanked the cowhands who'd helped him load up the cattle, slipped on his sunglasses, and climbed into the cab.

"Geronimo," he muttered as he put the Jeep in gear, and left Midland for Rascal and the Circle B.

A DISTANT CLOUD OF DUST SIGNALED THE ARRIVAL OF AN approaching vehicle. Savannah stopped hanging out diapers on the clothesline. She used cloth diapers and a clothesline both because it was better for the environment and it saved money, but it was a lot more work. Maybe she'd reconsider plastic diapers now that Ginger was gone.

She shaded her eyes against the bright, noonday sun beating down on her scalp. Yep. Someone was headed to the ranch. She wasn't expecting any visitors. Who could it be?

Her busy day had started at dawn when she'd helped Clem feed the livestock. Then they'd spent the next several hours cleaning up the garden area, littered with debris from the wedding.

Currently, Clem was in town buying supplies while she took care of the household chores. Cody napped in his playpen under the sheltering mimosa. Oh, how she missed Ginger.

She moved toward the driveway, smoothing her palms

down the front of her cutoff blue jeans, wiping away perspiration from her hands.

Matt's red Jeep flashed into view.

Her heart leapt with joy. As upset as she'd been with him the night before, she was so happy to see him. And then she noticed the cattle trailer. Was he bringing the Santa Gertrudis cattle home? Did that mean the sheriff no longer considered her a suspect?

Hope surged through her as she hurried to meet him.

He swung out of the Jeep and tipped his Stetson back on his head, a wide grin crossing his face. Savannah fought an almost irresistible urge to throw her arms around his neck and kiss him. She surrendered her right to do that two years ago when she'd broken up with him.

"Got you a present." He jerked a thumb at the trailer.

She moved to the back of the long vehicle and stood on tiptoe to peer inside. Wide cow eyes stared back at her. Relief flooded her, giddy as champagne bubbles. They were her cattle. Eight short, but six was better than nothing. She could sell them and get out of debt. Whew. Her white knight in shining Jeep had arrived.

"Oh, Matt." She breathed. "Thank you."

The fine lines flaring out from his eyes eased into happy crinkles. "Thought they might cheer you up."

"Oh, yes."

"I'll unload them," he said. "And then we need to talk."

Talk.

Yes. They most certainly needed to talk. But she wasn't sure she was ready to tell him the secret she'd been keeping for two long years.

He doffed his Stetson, held the hat over his chest, looked like a contrite cowboy. "I want to apologize for last night. You were absolutely correct. I had no right to drag your son through a chase."

Our son. Drop the "y" and "your" son became "our" son.

Savannah's pulse skipped. How she longed to say "our" to him the way she had last night to the sheriff.

"Sometimes," she said. "You're too intense for your own good, Matt."

"Ah, but intensity is what makes me a good detective. And a good lover," he added mischievously.

She ignored that last part, even though a heated flush flared up her neck. "One day that intensity you're so proud of could cost you your life."

"That's why you broke up with me."

She nodded, but it was a lie. His job was merely the excuse she'd given him.

"I can change, Savvy." His eyes seemed haunted.

Was he asking for a second chance?

Desperate hope grabbed hold of her. How badly she ached for a second chance, but when Matt learned she'd kept his son from him, could he ever forgive her?

"Are you hungry?" he asked. "I took the liberty of buying sandwiches. I remembered how much you enjoyed the meatball subs from Parelli's."

Her stomach grumbled at the idea of Parelli's spicy meatball sandwiches. Matt knew her weaknesses far too well.

"What say we unload the cattle and then have a picnic?"

"I'm pretty busy," she hedged because his proposition sounded so romantic, and she couldn't afford romance. Not when she was carrying such a big secret.

"Too busy for one of Parelli's specialties? Oozing tomato sauce and mozzarella cheese?" he tempted.

Her mouth watered.

"Overflowing with sautéed onions and green bell peppers," he tantalized.

"No fair." She laughed. "Food warfare."

"All's fair in love and war," he quipped.

"And which is this, Matt?" she asked.

Their eyes met.

"War," they exclaimed in unison.

Laughing, they put the sandwiches in the refrigerator, woke Cody from his nap, and took him with them as they drove the cattle to the back pasture. It felt so nice. The three of them together like a family.

Savannah yearned. If only they could be.

"I don't know if this is the best place to keep the cattle." Savannah fretted, kneading her brow with her fingers. "I don't have a new lock for the gate, and the thieves removed them pretty easily the first time."

"Don't replace the lock. We want them easy to steal."

"I don't understand."

"I'll tell you all about it over lunch."

"Am I free to sell the Gerts?"

Matt backed the trailer across the rough terrain. "I'm sorry, but no."

"Why not? I've got the tax people chewing my behind for overdue property taxes, and I've got to do something."

"Stop worrying," he told her. "If my plan works, we'll have the thieves under arrest before you know it, and then you'll be free to do whatever you wish with the herd. And I intend on getting the rest of the cattle back for you, too."

"I certainly hope so." She got out of the truck and followed Matt to the back of the trailer, Cody settled comfortably at her hip.

Matt let the trailer door down, and he stepped aside. The cattle jostled each other getting out of the trailer and into the pasture.

"Da." Cody pointed at the cows and made grasping motions with his hand.

"Cows," Savannah instructed. She took his hand and rubbed it against the neck of the docile animal. "Moo."

Cody giggled and bucked joyfully in her arms. "Cow!"

"Yes, cows." She laughed. Finally, he'd said something besides "da." She'd started worrying about his lack of verbal skills.

"Cow, cow, cow," Cody sang.

"He's a little cowboy already," Matt murmured.

She looked up and caught Matt studying them with a pensive expression on his face. His gaze caught hers, and he gave her a look so weighted with meaning that Savannah gulped. Was he feeling the same gut-churning emotions that she was? Did the same yearning to recapture what they'd lost hang heavy in his chest?

"Mission accomplished," he said, his tone as light as butterfly wings. "Let's head to the house and those sandwiches. I'm starving."

"Me, too."

They returned to the farmhouse and washed up. Savannah packed a picnic basket with the sandwiches, baby food for Cody, fresh fruit and potato chips, and filled a cooler with apple juice and soft drinks.

"Where are we going?" she asked.

"It's your ranch. You pick the spot."

"Morgan's Meadow," she said, naming the spot named after Gary's great-grandfather. "By the creek. We can let Cody go wading."

"Sounds great."

"Let's walk," she said. "It isn't far. Just over the hill and down in the valley a bit. About half a mile."

She reapplied sunscreen to her face and arms, then slathered a coating over Cody's wiggly little body. She put on a straw hat as a shield against the Texas noonday sun and settled a tiny baseball cap on her son's head.

Matt shouldered the picnic basket and cooler. Savannah tucked the blanket under one arm and held Cody in the other. Matt opened the back door, and they traipsed out across the pasture.

Mockingbirds and scissortails flitted through the mesquite and chinaberry trees. Wildflowers swayed in the fields—orange-red Indian paintbrushes, yellow black-eyed Susan, purple prickly pears. Grasshoppers leaped beneath their feet.

The delicious aroma of garlicky meatballs seeped up from the wooden picnic basket. Bees hummed by. Butterflies pirouetted in the air. In the distance, a creek gurgled. They topped the hill and started down into the valley. A narrow stream ran through a clump of chinaberry trees. Savannah pointed out the spot.

"Let's picnic here."

Matt set the picnic basket and cooler underneath the shade of the tree, took the blanket from Savannah, and spread it on the ground.

She sank to her knees and placed the toddler beside her on the blanket. Cody squealed with delight and played with toy firetruck she'd brought along to distract him.

"Since he seems content right now, why don't we eat first, and I'll feed him later," Savannah said.

"Whatever you say, you're the mom." He studied her. "You're a great mother, by the way."

His kind words hurt because would a great mother have kept a father from his son?

You had good reasons for doing what you did.

But what had seemed good reasons at the time, now felt like excuses. Shouldn't she have at least given Matt a chance to make up his own mind instead of deciding everything for him? Even if she did have his best interest at heart by breaking up with him. She feared he wasn't going to see it that way when he learned the truth.

Guilt was a sledgehammer, knocking against her chest.

Matt sat down next to her, doffed his hat, and ran a hand through his hair. He looked so handsome, she could scarcely catch her breath.

"I'll warn you right now, moms rarely get through a meal without being interrupted," she said.

"I can handle that. As long as I'm with you, I can handle anything." Then he lightly touched her forearm, and Savannah just about came undone.

❧ 11 ❧

Matt couldn't help noticing that Savannah gently moved her arm away and couldn't meet his gaze. Did she feel as overwhelmed as he did by the powerful attraction that hadn't lessened one whit in two years apart? It had, if anything, grown stronger.

She leaned over and opened the picnic basket. Her luscious hair feathered over her high cheekbones. Her vanilla scent tickled his nose. Her little bell earrings tinkled softly. A lump formed in his throat.

What in the Sam Hill was he doing here? Matt closed his eyes and remembered other picnics, other events where they'd stretched out on a blanket together. Those times had ended in wild embraces, with arms and legs tangled together, their mouths molded around each other.

Matt swallowed hard. A picnic had been a stupid idea.

"Here you go," she said.

He opened his eyes to see her smiling at him. The sight took his breath. She tucked a strand of hair behind a delicate ear, extending the wax-paper-wrapped sandwich toward him.

"Th...th...thanks," he stuttered, so thrown by her beauty he just stared.

"Need something to drink?" she asked.

"Yes," he croaked.

"Soda or apple juice?"

"Whatever."

She pulled the tab on a cola can and handed him the cold soft drink. He pressed it to his forehead in an attempt to cool the heat raging within him. Wow. He had to get hold of himself, and pronto.

Unwrapping her own sandwich, Savannah held it gingerly between her fingers so the tomato sauce wouldn't drip on her clothes. Her mouth opened. Matt saw a flash of her friendly pink tongue, and he groaned inwardly.

She took a cautious bite.

Matt had to glance away, his own sandwich growing clammy in his sweaty palm. He tried to concentrate on eating but could think of nothing except Savannah's mouth, her tongue, her sweet, full lips.

"Arg." He sighed.

"Something wrong?"

She swallowed the bite of meatball sandwich and stared at him with wide gold-green eyes. A spot of tomato sauce dotted the corner of her mouth. Matt fought the urge to lean over and kiss it away. She saved him by dabbing it off with a napkin.

He shook his head.

Cody scooted across the blanket between them. Grateful for the distraction, Matt turned his attention to the baby. Cody reached for Matt's sandwich, and he broke off a chunk of bread and offered it to him. The boy drooled on the tidbit and grinned.

"Chips?" Savannah held up the bag.

Matt shook his head.

"French onion," she tempted. "Your favorite."

"You remembered."

"I remember a lot of things about you."

Same here. Too darn many things, like how her breasts felt pressed against his chest, and the way she loved to have her tummy tickled with a light, gentle touch. Had Markum catered to her desires? He didn't even want to think about her and Markum together. Even though the man was dead, jealousy still knotted his chest.

"So," Savannah said, licking the sauce from her fingers. "Tell me about your plans to catch the cattle thieves."

Matt set his sandwich aside, too keyed up to eat another bite. He stretched out on the blanket, cradled his head in his palms, and stared through the tree branches at the cerulean sky. Cody crawled over his belly and sat right on his chest.

"Come here, Cody," Savannah said, clapping her hands. "Get off Matt."

"He's okay," Matt assured her and wrapped an arm around the boy.

Savannah popped open a jar of baby food, and that got Cody's attention fast. He slid off Matt and reached for his mother.

"I thought that might convince you," she cooed.

Matt narrowed his eyes, lazily watching mother and child.

"So go ahead," Savannah said while angling a spoonful of strained apricots into Cody's eager mouth.

"I know you're not going to want to hear this, but I think Clem might be involved," Matt said.

Savannah frowned. "Why?"

"Think about it, Savvy. How did the thieves get in and out so quickly? That west pasture is a far piece from the house. They had to have at least two trailers for fourteen head of cattle or one mighty big one. How come nobody heard anything?"

She shrugged, wiping Cody's chin with a napkin. "They still could have managed it without Clem's help."

Matt raised a palm. "I have a theory."

"Let's hear it."

"What if Clem knew about the insurance policy?"

"Suppose he did. So what? How would he benefit from that?" She glanced at him, lips pursed in an inquisitive pucker.

His heart jackhammered. Good grief, what was happening to him? Two years ago, she'd hurt him so badly he thought he'd never recover, and now one look from her and he felt like a schoolboy on his first date, angling to slip his arm around a pretty girl at the movies.

"Clem wouldn't benefit from the insurance policy, but he realizes you will."

"Yes?" Her hair swung against her shoulders.

"Yeah. He doesn't feel guilty about stealing the cattle knowing you'll get the insurance money. He knows you're in tough financial straits. In fact, he might see it as a way to solve both your troubles. He gets a cut on the profits from the thefts, and you get the insurance money."

Savannah gnawed her thumbnail. "I can't believe it of Clem. He's worked for Gary's family for over twenty years."

"What about Todd? He drew up the policy for Gary, and yet, when you told him your cattle were missing, he never once mentioned the policy. That's suspicious, too," Matt pointed out.

"Todd? No way. He's so honest, he squeaks. He's been thinking about the wedding, not business. I'm sure it just slipped his mind."

"So we're back to Clem."

"But why?"

"Maybe he starts considering the idea of stealing your cattle after the other thefts occurred. Then he's thinking if your cattle turn up missing, the sheriff will assume it's the same culprits."

"I guess it's a possibility."

"And then there's this. A few days ago, I saw him in Kelly's with Brent Larkins and Hootie Thompson, two of the most unsavory characters this side of the Pecos."

❧

SAVANNAH DIDN'T LIKE WHAT MATT WAS SAYING. SHE didn't want to believe that Clem was capable of such a thing. He'd been so good to her since Gary's death. His advanced age prevented him from doing more, but she'd always believed he possessed a kind heart. Now, Matt's words had her doubting her own judgment.

Was she really so blind?

Scraping the last spoonful of apricots from the jar, she fed Cody the remaining bite, then wiped his mouth again. Then she peeled a banana, broke off half, and gave it to him. He squeezed the banana between his chubby fingers and laughed.

"But you don't have any solid evidence, correct?" Her eyes met Matt's.

He propped himself up on one elbow, stuck a blade of grass between his teeth, and nodded. "If we want to catch him, we've got to set a trap."

"You think he'd do it again?"

"If not him, then Larkins and Thompson."

Savannah shook her head. "I don't know about this."

"You want to get the rest of your cattle back?"

"Well, sure, but will this do the trick?"

"Worth a try."

"I suppose." She shrugged and let out a long sigh.

"I want to close this case."

She looked away to see Cody toddling toward the creek.

Moving quickly, she intercepted him before he could dive headfirst into the water.

He squealed his displeasure and flailed his arms at her.

"Okay, okay, I'll let you wade for a minute." Ignoring Matt, she squatted next to the creek, held Cody under his arms, and let him splash his feet in the cool stream that trickled down from the snow off the Davis Mountains in the spring.

"Remember the time we drove to Turner Falls in Oklahoma?" Matt's voice rumbled, husky and low, across the prairie.

Savannah squeezed her eyes shut. Why was he doing this to her? Torturing her with memories, with regrets, with thoughts of what might have been.

"Remember?" he repeated.

Boy, did she ever.

That trip to Turner Falls had been the most exotic, erotic adventure of her young life. Matt had borrowed his uncle's new pickup, and they'd packed a tent and supplies. During the entire journey, she'd practically sat in his lap, Matt's arms curving around her to reach the steering wheel while she rested her head against his chest.

They'd laughed and talked and sung along with the radio. She'd felt so loved, so cared for. Back when she was young and stupid and still believed in happily ever after.

Once at Turner Falls, they'd been delighted to discover the park almost deserted at that time of year. It was late September and kids were in school. They pitched the tent, then spent the afternoon climbing the craggy rocks, exploring the caves, and swimming in the clear water pools. They'd cooked hot dogs over an open fire, then kissed beneath a waterfall, long, slow, and tender.

Warmth suffused her solar plexus as she remembered the feel of Matt's callused fingers skimming her pliant body, the hungry taste of his thirsty mouth, the sound of water splattering around them. Only the unexpected arrival of park rangers had kept them from making love on that trip.

The memory made her shiver.

Cody giggled, splashing cold water in her face.

Savannah opened her eyes. Matt crouched beside her. Her gaze floated up to meet his.

"When did things go so wrong between us?" he asked.

Cody plunked down on his bottom in the stream. Savannah wrapped her arms around her knees, her straw hat hiding her face from him.

"Savvy?"

She turned her head and eyed him. The thin scar on the side of his face, courtesy of Julio Diaz's knife, had gone from red to dull pink. That scar epitomized Matt. He was relentless. Nothing ever got in his way. He would move heaven and earth to achieve his goals.

Tell him about Cody.

She opened her mouth. "Matt, I...there's something you should know."

"About the cattle?"

Savannah stood up abruptly, picked Cody up, and took him back to the blanket for a diaper change. Her chest tightened as if twisted in a vise. It was so hard to open herself up to the hurt and anger she knew that was coming. Was this really the best place with Cody crawling underfoot?

You're stalling.

Yes, she was.

"Savannah?"

She heard him get to his feet and felt him come up behind her as she put Cody on his back and changed his diaper.

"Honey? What's wrong?" He placed a hand on her shoulder. His touch sent a tremor throughout her body.

She shrugged him off. She didn't deserve his tenderness.

She finished up with the diaper change and gave Cody a cookie to keep him occupied.

"Talk to me, Savvy."

"I..." Oh God, just *say* it.

"You can tell me anything, sweetheart," he whispered.

"Anything?" She stared into his steady gaze. Did he somehow suspect?

"Anything." He nodded. "I won't judge you."

"What happened between us two years ago—"

"Is over," he said firmly. "We don't have to talk about it. The past is the past." He took her hand in his. "What I want to talk about is our future."

"Our fu...future?" she stammered.

"Ever since I saw you again I've felt the old pull, stronger than ever." He brushed away a lock of hair from her cheek. "And I think you feel it, too."

She did! "Things aren't that simple, Matt."

"Sure they are. Or they could be. I still love you, and I'm praying hard that you love me, too."

She closed her eyes, swallowing hard past the lump in her throat. "There are things you don't understand."

This was so difficult. She was about to filet herself wide open, leaving her heart bare.

He cupped her chin in his palm, tilting her face up to meet his gaze. "If only you could curb this irrational fear of yours that I'll end up getting killed, then maybe we might have a chance to rebuild something together. I know you've had a lot of loss in your life, that it's hard for you to trust—"

"It's not that."

"What is it then?"

Tears sprang to her eyes as she remembered that night at Kelly's. Matt had taken her out on a date to celebrate his acceptance into specialized law enforcement training in El

Paso. The news had shattered her because he would be gone for months.

At the bar, an outburst between two drunken cowboys fighting over the female bartender, Jackie Spencer, had drawn Matt's attention. Characteristically, Matt had intervened. One of the cowboys had pulled a gun. They tussled. And Matt ended up getting shot in the arm. The memory echoed in her brain—the fear, the agony, the apprehension, followed by sheer gratitude that he was alive.

Carried on a river of emotion, they'd made love when he was released from the hospital. What a bittersweet time that turned out to be.

"Remember the night we made love?"

Matt's eyes narrowed, darkened. "Remember it? I think about it every single day. I thought I'd found my one and only. I thought we were on our road to happily-ever-after and then you pulled the rug out from under me."

Savannah had thought that too, but life had other plans.

"I can't get you out of my head. For the past two years, there's been no one else. I had a few dates, but no one could compare to you. I haven't..." He gulped visibly. "Been with anyone else since we broke up."

He hadn't made love to another woman since her? Savannah put a hand to her throat. She thought about mentioning that she'd seen him with Jackie Spencer when she drove to El Paso to tell him she was pregnant, but she wasn't ready to reveal that quite yet. Had she really gotten it wrong? He'd led Jackie into his apartment...

"While you," His voice deepened. "Well, you married Gary, didn't you? How long was it before you hopped from my bed into his? A month?"

"It wasn't like that between Gary and me, Matt."

"What was it like, Savvy? How could you run so hot for me one minute, then turn so cold the next? You claimed it was my job, but you'd made peace with what I did for a living before then. Just because I got shot breaking up a bar fight—"

"You could have been killed."

"Still, you made love to me after that fight, when I got out of the hospital. If you had such doubts, wouldn't me getting shot have been the deal-breaker? Instead, you waited until after we had sex to break up with me. For the past two years, I haven't been able to puzzle that out. What made you go from making love to me to dumping me, to marrying Gary? It was impulsive and erratic, and not like you in the least. You wouldn't take my calls, wouldn't answer my texts, wouldn't give me a chance to make things right. I would have changed my career for you."

"I couldn't let you do that." There was truth to that. She could not ask him to give up the job he loved for her. It wouldn't have been fair to either one of them.

"Help me understand, Savannah because I really want to know so that I don't blow it with you a second time. What did I do that was so wrong?" The anguish on his face tore a hole in her heart.

"You didn't do anything wrong, Matt. You're not to blame." She shifted from foot to foot, her stomaching tightening.

"Then who is to blame? Tell me, Savannah. Tell me what happened."

"Do you want to know what happened?"

"I do. Please, tell me what went wrong. The not knowing has driven me crazy for two long years."

She looked him in the eyes. She felt as if she wanted to crawl right out of her own skin. Here it was. The secret she'd been keeping from him. The time was now. No more dodging. Truth will out.

"It wasn't like that between Gary and me..." Moistening

her lips, she managed to croak past the constriction in her throat. "Because we never had sex."

"What do you mean?" Matt blinked as the information hit him. "You have a baby. How could you have a baby if you and Gary didn't have sex?"

"That night you and I made love?" A surge of courage pushed through her, and she finally told him what she should have told him two years ago. "I got pregnant."

12

The news rocked Matt to his core. He stood there with his mouth hanging open.

Savannah had gotten pregnant the night they made love? With his baby? Cody was *their* child?

"Cody," he rasped, stunned. "Is *my* son?"

She wrapped her arms around her as if warding off blows. Nodding, she whispered, "He is your son."

Gobsmacked, Matt's knees gave way, and he dropped to the blanket, his butt hitting the ground. *I have a son.*

The first emotion to hit him was deep, intense joy.

I have a son.

The second wave of emotion was disbelief.

I have a *son*?

The third was shock.

I *have* a son.

By the time he'd started fully processing the information, reality seeped in. I have a *fifteen-month-old* son.

All this time, Savannah had known he had a son, and she'd kept the information from him.

The fourth lick of emotion was hurt. How could she not

tell him? Followed quickly by anger. *What the hell, Savvy? What the hell?*

"Matt?" She wrung her hands. "Are you okay?"

He stared up at her, slowly shook his head, and drilled her with his gaze. "No," he said. "I'm not okay. I'm not okay at all. Not by a long shot."

Tears glistened in her eyes, and she'd knotted her fingers together. She was hurting, too.

Well, she should, the contrary side of him said. She was in the wrong. "Why didn't you tell me?" he ground out the words through clenched teeth and popped to his feet. He crossed his arms and loomed over her.

Her bottom lip trembled, her shoulders slumped, and all the fight went out of him.

He wanted to pull her into his arms and comfort her. Savannah was not a cruel person. If she'd kept his son from him, he felt sure she'd had a good reason. Although right now, he couldn't fathom why.

They stared at each other.

"Life is full of unexpected events. We make our choices, right or wrong, and we live with them," she said.

He tightened his jaw, his body wired with adrenaline spilling through his bloodstream. "Yes, and Cody and I are living with *your* choices."

"Let me explain."

He clenched his jaw so hard it hurt, trying to hold onto his anger. "I'm listening."

The weighted topic was too heavy for such a lighthearted, bucolic location. Picnic by the creek, desert mountain in the distance.

She pressed a hand to her mouth, her eyes haunted. Her hair curled down her long, slender neck. Matt quelled the sudden urge to lean over and feather a kiss on that cool, white spot. Would he ever stop desiring her?

If only he could let go! For two years, he'd tried to accept her rejection, and for a while, he thought he'd accomplished that goal. He'd dated other women, but nobody special. He'd thrown himself into his work and had risen rapidly through the hierarchy. He'd always known he wanted to stay in the field, had shunned any thoughts of a desk position, but now, looking at Savannah, his mind toyed with the idea.

What if he, Savannah, and Cody could become a real family?

The yearning was so intense, it almost knocked him down again.

When she said nothing, he took the bull by the horns. "You used my job, the fact that I got shot, to break up with me."

She nodded, her eyes swimming with unshed tears. "Your job *is* dangerous."

"But you could accept that."

"I had to. It's who you are," she said. "I knew it was part of the package of loving Matt Forrester."

Loving.

So she *had* loved him, even though she'd never said it back to him. Did she love him still? That battered old hope kicked around in him again. He loved her more than ever, but that didn't lessen the pain of her betrayal.

Cody sat on the blanket, gnawing on a cookie, and beaming up at them with his beautiful baby smile. He had no idea about the drama going on above him. It was all Matt could do not to scoop the child into his arms and just walk away with him. Let her see what the loss felt like. But of course, he could not hurt her like that.

He looked down at the boy, and his heart just broke. He'd missed Savannah's pregnancy, Cody's birth, all those little firsts. First smile. First tooth. First word. First steps.

Cheated. He'd been cheated.

"Why?" The word tore from his throat like a war cry. "Why?"

Savannah hitched in a breath, her hands clenched at her sides, her entire body shuddering at the force of her inhale. "After you got shot, the day after we made love, I discovered I carried the BRCA1 gene."

"The what?" Confused, he scratched his head.

"The hereditary breast cancer gene that killed my mother. I've got it."

Matt's blood instantly ran cold. Fear rocked his spine. "What does that mean?"

"Inheriting the BRCA gene means I have close to a seventy-five percent chance of developing breast cancer and close to a fifty-percent chance of getting ovarian cancer." Savannah sounded so calm. "I didn't know it ran in our family because my mother was adopted. It was only after she got diagnosed that we found out."

"I… I…" He had no idea what to say. To mumble that he was sorry seemed woefully inadequate. She'd been hiding this from him for two years. "I didn't know that's the kind of breast cancer your mother had." He rubbed his brow. "I didn't know you got tested."

"I didn't want to worry you." She stuck her hands in her pockets and toed the blanket with her bare foot. "You were getting ready to take that training in El Paso."

"You should have told me."

"Would you have gone to El Paso if I had?"

He shook his head.

"Don't you see? I couldn't be the one who stopped you from going after your dreams."

"Don't you think that should have been my decision to make?"

"I was watching my mother die of breast cancer. I couldn't, wouldn't put you through that with me."

"Again, that was my decision to make." It felt as if she'd inserted a giant screwdriver into the center of his chest, twisting it as far as it would go.

"We weren't married, Matt. I could not ask that of you."

"We would have been married if you hadn't shut me out."

She shook her head. "I didn't shut you out, Matt. I set you free."

"Let me get this straight," he said, unable to keep the anger from his voice. "You sent me away for my own good because you loved me too much to marry me?"

"Yes."

"I'm guessing the same didn't apply to Gary?"

"As I said, my relationship with Gary wasn't like that."

"What was it like, Savvy?" he repeated.

Regret flittered across her face. "I'm getting to that. My doctor urged me to have a bilateral mastectomy and a hysterectomy as soon as possible. The surgeries would greatly increase my chances for long-term survival, and I needed to be here for Ginger. She'd tested negative for the BRCA1 gene. I couldn't put her through what we went through with Mom. I was all prepared to have the surgery—"

"This was right after you broke up with me?"

"Yes."

He'd been in El Paso, drowning his sorrows in his training while she'd been here dealing with her health crisis. He'd been feeling sorry for himself while the woman he loved had been struggling. He was an ass.

But you didn't know.

He should have known. He should have tried harder. Should have fought to find out why she'd really broken up with him instead of tucking his tail between his legs and high-tailing it out of Rascal to nurse his hurt feelings. At the time, the detective training in El Paso had been a godsend, and then the police department had offered him a job afterward, so he'd just stayed.

"Why didn't you call me? I would have been there in a shot."

"One, you were in the middle of your training, and I didn't want to interrupt that—"

"I want the *real* reason," he growled.

She ducked her head, mumbled, "I was afraid you wouldn't want me without my breasts, without my ovaries. You deserve a whole woman, Matt."

"It was awfully high-handed of you to decide what was right for me. To decide what *I* deserved."

"I didn't feel worthy of you, okay? I had a dying mother and a scary prognosis for my own future. I was going to lose the parts of me that made me feminine. I was struggling with body issues, okay?"

"So you had the surgery?" His gaze dropped to her breasts, his heart in his throat.

She nodded. "But not then. When I went in for testing before the surgery, they discovered I was pregnant."

Aw hell, the poor girl. "*That's* when you should have called me, Savannah." His voice came out gritty and dark. "Why didn't you come to find me when you learned you were pregnant?"

She looked utterly wretched. "I did."

"When?" He wrapped his hand around her upper arm, pulled her closer, and drilled her with his eyes.

"A month after you left. I got in the car and drove to El Paso. I looked up your address, parked on the street and waited for you to come home. And you did. With Jackie Spencer. I saw you two together. You put a hand to her back and guided her into your apartment."

Matt groaned. Tasted bile. He had let Jackie live with him for a few weeks when she moved to El Paso until she could find a place of her own, but he had not slept with her. Although it wasn't from lack of trying on Jackie's part. He'd just been too in love with Savannah to give up hope. He supposed he'd never given up hope. He had no idea what she'd been dealing with.

"Jackie was staying with me, but we weren't together. I did not sleep with her, Savannah."

Her eyes widened, and her mouth formed a startled O. "Really?"

"Really." God, his emotions were all over the place—regret, shame, sadness, hurt, yearning, but at the bottom of them, all was hope. Hope that they could repair the mess they'd made of their relationship.

He saw the same hope on her in the way she leaned closer and pulled her bottom lip up between her teeth.

"So, Gary," he said, his breathing ragged. "What was that all about?"

"I met Gary at a cancer support group with Mom. He guessed I was pregnant when I kept running to the bathroom to throw up, and he didn't believe my food poisoning excuse. He was so sweet and kind. Then he offered me a proposition. Marry him and give him a legacy. He was dying. He had no one except his half-brother, who was in prison for murder. He didn't want sex from me. He just wanted someone to be there with him in the end. His only request was that I let people believe that Cody was his son." This time she couldn't stop the tears from rolling down her cheeks.

"You cared for Gary."

"I wouldn't have made it without him. Mom died not long after that. Ginger and I moved to the ranch. Gary paid for everything."

His heart was breaking right in two for her. For what she'd had to go through. "You eventually had the bilateral mastectomy and your ovaries removed?"

Nodding, she placed a hand to her lower abdomen. "The last surgery was six months ago."

"Oh, Savvy," he said. "I am so sorry. I should have been there."

"It was my fault. My stubborn pride. When I saw you with Jackie Spencer, I sort of lost my mind."

"I was pigheaded, too. Hurt and feeling sorry for myself. I should have checked on you. Especially when I heard your mother died. I—"

Cody started crying.

"Too much sun for one day," she murmured and looked relieved for the interruption. "It's time for his nap."

He wanted to reach out to her, draw her to his chest, kiss her like he did when they were younger, but there was too much between them to bridge that gap so easily. He hadn't been there for her, even though he hadn't known how badly she needed him. She hadn't trusted him enough to come to him, no matter what.

And that was the bottom line, wasn't it? The shakiness of trust between them. They had desire, attraction, and yearning. Oh, so much damn yearning, but without trust, they did not have a foundation to build upon.

If they were to find their way back to each it other, it was going to take time. He couldn't rush it.

"May I carry him?" he asked, reaching for Cody.

Silently, she nodded and handed him his son.

Matt stared at the boy. Cody studied him with a serious expression on his face as if trying to puzzle out who he was. "I'm your Dad," Matt said.

"Da?" Cody asked.

"Da," Matt confirmed with a nod of his head.

"Dada?" Cody reached out to pat his cheek. "Dada."

Matt glanced over at Savannah. She dabbed away tears with a napkin she'd packed for the sandwiches. He wanted to say something that could make it all better, but there were no magic words to fix this.

They trailed back to the house, forlornly dragging their supplies with them. Even Cody sensed the mood. He whimpered and rubbed his eyes with tired little fists. The perky atmosphere that had started the afternoon dissipated, scattered to the wind like dandelion seeds.

13

As they neared the house, Matt spotted Clem loping between the barn and the ranch hands' cabin. A half-formed plan hatched in the back of his mind. A plan to use Clem as a foil to trap Larkins and Thompson. His instincts told him those two career criminals were behind the thefts, and Clem was merely a pawn.

A very useful pawn.

"Savvy," he said. "You take Cody and go on into the house. Clem and I are going to have a discussion."

She started to protest, he could see it in the stubborn tilt of her chin, but she must have thought better of it because she finally nodded. Setting down the empty picnic basket, she took her son from his arms.

"I want you to play along with me, all right? No matter what I say."

"Matt..." She hesitated, concern reflected in her wide eyes. "Clem isn't a bad person."

"Do you trust me?" He watched her eyes for the truth. He was talking about much more than what he was going to say to Clem.

Her nod was quick, brief. "I'll back you up."

"Does Clem know I took you in for questioning last night?" he asked.

"Not that I know of. I haven't discussed anything with him this morning."

"Good." Matt tugged the brim of his Stetson lower on his forehead. "Get prepared to be arrested."

"What?" Her mouth dropped. "I thought you believed me!"

"Just play along." He inclined his head toward the house. "Go on inside. I'll be back in a minute."

Savannah disappeared into the house. Matt cocked his shoulder and put on his most serious lawman stance. He stalked across the yard and rapped sharply on the cabin door.

A corner of the curtain fluttered.

Matt knocked again. Waited. "Clem, I saw you go in there. This is Detective Matt Forrester. Open the door."

A minute later, the door creaked open. Clem peeked out like a furtive mouse, a cigarette butt clutched between nicotine-stained fingers.

"Whatcha want?" the older man asked, narrowing his eyes.

Matt remembered how the man had avoided him yesterday at Ginger's wedding. Olson knew something about the missing cattle. Matt had no doubts about it.

Slicker than a door-to-door peddler, Matt inserted the toe of his boot inside the door. "May I come in?"

Clem scratched his chest. He wore a dirty T-shirt and even dirtier blue jeans. A day's worth of grizzled whiskers ran the length of his jaw. His eyes were tired and bloodshot. He looked like a man hiding secrets.

"Don't suppose I can refuse a lawman, can I?"

"I'd appreciate your time," Matt said evenly.

Clem stepped aside. "Come on in then."

The older man shut the door behind him. Matt blinked, adjusting to the cabin's dim light. The room was as unkempt as the ranch hand, a far different sight than when Matt had searched it looking for Julio Diaz. Obviously, Clem hadn't cleaned the cabin since then. Empty beer bottles staggered around the overflowing trash can. Dirty dishes were piled in the sink. Bits of debris littered the floor.

"Did you catch them cattle thieves yet?" Clem asked.

"We don't know who physically took the cattle, but we do know who instigated the whole thing." Matt crowded Clem's personal space. He intended on scaring the old man into running back to Larkins and Thompson with the story.

Clem's hand trembled as he raised it to touch his chin. "You do?"

Matt nodded solemnly. "Yep, and it's tearing my heart out to have to arrest her."

"Her?" Clem's voice went up an octave.

Matt smiled inwardly. Aha. The fish had taken the bait. "Savannah. We figure she hired some goons to take off with her cattle so she could cash in on the insurance money."

"Miss Savannah?" Clem gulped, his Adam's apple bobbing.

"Never would have thought it possible." Matt shook his head, feigning shock. "But we've got the evidence. I'm about to take her in right now. Just wanted to let you know because it might affect your living arrangements."

Clem's tremors increased. He fumbled in his pocket for a pack of cigarettes. "What about Cody?"

"Sad. We'll give Ginger a chance to claim him, but failing that, he'll go into the foster care system."

Clem looked stunned. "I thought you and Miss Savannah used to be friendly."

"That was a long time ago, Clem."

"I still can't believe you'd treat her this way."

"She's a suspect."

Clem's eyes narrowed. "Miss Savannah was right."

"About what?" Matt frowned.

Clem's top lip curled in disgust. "'Bout you. I overheard her talking to Miss Ginger the night before the wedding. Told her she still loved you, but that she was a fool. Said you couldn't ever love no flesh-and-blood woman because you were too in love with your gun and badge." Clem spit on the floor at Matt's feet. "Guess she was right."

The old man's words hit Matt like a sledgehammer blow. Was it really true? Savannah still in love with him after all these years?

How he wanted to believe.

Touching his hat with his fingertips, Matt moved for the door. "I'm on my way to arrest her now. Thought you might like to know."

"You can't do that." Clem pressed his body against the door, blocking Matt's way. Sweat dripped down the ranch hand's face.

"Why not?"

Clem hesitated.

Matt sank his hands on his hips. "Something you want to tell me?"

Clem cussed at him.

Ignoring the onslaught, Matt shouldered the old man aside, pushed through the door, and walked toward the farmhouse. His heart thudded like a percussion drum in an echo chamber. He had to make the show good for Clem's sake. He hoped what was left of the old man's cowboy ethics would kick in, and he'd hightail it straight to Larkins and Thompson and demand they do something to exonerate Savannah.

When he reached the back door, he rapped on it sharply. "Mrs. Markum," he shouted. He felt more than saw Clem lope up behind him. He withdrew handcuffs from his back pocket and dangled them for Clem's benefit. "This is Detective Forrester."

Savannah pulled open the door, Cody on her hip.

"Step out on the porch and give me the baby." Matt winked broadly at her where Clem couldn't see.

Silently, Savannah handed the baby to him.

"Turn around and put your hands behind you."

She did as he instructed. When he wrapped the cuffs around her slender wrists, the clicking noise almost killed him. Even though it was make-believe, the image burned in Matt's brain. Savannah's warm, slender hands held captive by cold, cruel metal.

"You have the right to remain silent," he began the spiel. *Oh, Lord*, he prayed, *let Clem fall for the scheme.*

"Detective!" Clem sang out.

Matt froze. Slowly, he turned, Cody clutched in his arms. "You got something to tell me, Clem?"

"Let her go. Miss Savannah didn't have nothin' to do with them cows disappearing."

"How would you know that, Clem?"

"I know who did steal 'em." The old man took a deep breath, thrusting out his bony chest.

A confession. It wasn't what he'd expected, but it would work just as well. Matt fished in his pocket for the key to the handcuffs and removed them from Savannah's wrists.

"Okay, Clem," Matt said, "suppose you tell me what you know."

Savannah took Cody from Matt's arms, then glanced from him to Clem and back again.

Clem looked uncomfortable. "Remember that afternoon you saw me in Kelly's with Hootie Thompson and Brent Larkins?"

Matt nodded, waiting.

Ducking his head, Clem drew a circle in the dirt with the

tip of his boot. "I lied to you when I said they was only buying me a beer."

"Go on."

"I owed 'em gambling money."

"What has that got to do with my missing Gerts?" Savannah asked.

Matt quelled her with one strong stare. Savannah snapped her mouth closed.

"And you couldn't pay the debt. Is that correct, Clem?"

The ranch hand nodded.

"You knew Gary had taken out an insurance policy on the Santa Gertrudis herd and that if they were to come up missing, it would only help Savannah since she was having financial trouble. So you planted the seed of stealing cattle in Larkins's brain to extricate yourself from his debt, didn't you?"

"No, sir," Clem denied hotly. "It was their idea. They said they would let me off the hook if I got them onto the ranch and helped them steal Savannah's Gerts. Because of those other thefts, Larkins thought the sheriff would figure it was the same hombres that hit the Circle B." Clem pulled a wry face. "Guess they didn't figure on you, huh?"

"I guess not," Matt said.

"Anyway," Clem continued. "I never meant to get Miss Savannah in trouble. Like you said, I thought the insurance money would help her pay the property taxes and cover Ginger's wedding expenses."

"Well, that doesn't quite cut it, does it, Clem?" Matt cocked his head to one side, staring down the elderly man.

"I'm sorry, Miss Savannah," Clem mumbled.

"You think an apology is enough for what you put her through?" Matt asked.

"No. But you'll be arresting me instead."

"Not necessarily." Matt stroked his jaw with a thumb and

forefinger. "Not if you'd be willing to cooperate with the sheriff's department."

"What do you want?" Clem asked, jumping at the chance to make amends for his mistake.

"Help me snare Larkins and Thompson."

"With pleasure." Clem rubbed his palms together. "Just tell me what to do."

Matt threw an arm around the older man's shoulders. "Here's the plan."

❧

"You're coming to stay at my place," Matt told Savannah fifteen minutes later.

Clem had been dispatched into Rascal to find Larkins and Thompson to put Matt's plan into action. After cooking supper, Savannah had fed Cody, put him to bed, and now she stood at the sink washing dishes.

"No, I'm not. Cody needs to be in his home."

"Don't be pigheaded, Savannah. I'm not leaving you alone in the house as long as Larkins and Thompson are on the loose, believing that you are in jail and the ranch is unprotected. Mark my words, they'll be back to steal the rest of your Gerts." He was sitting at her kitchen table, cleaning his gun. He wore a white cotton undershirt and jeans, the leather holster strapped around his shoulder, his shirt thrown over the back of a chair.

She let the sudsy water out of the sink, then dried her hands on a dish towel. "This was your plan. Not mine."

"All right, then," he replied. "If you won't come to my place, I'll put you up in a motel."

"Do you have any idea what a production it is to transport a fifteen-month-old? You're talking diaper bags and baby food, the Pack 'n Play, and toys. No." She crossed her arms, raised her chin, and stared him straight in the eye, daring him to contradict her. "There's only one logical option. You'll have to stay here."

"You're right," he said. "That is a better plan."

The idea of Matt spending the night in her home had Savannah's pulse skipping. "Do you think they'll make a move tonight?"

"They might, and I'll be here to see it through to the end."

"Do you think things could get violent?" She braced herself for his answer.

"I'm not taking any chances," he said grimly. "Not where you and Cody are concerned."

Matt was the epitome of a tough, rugged lawman—fierce, cagey, vigilant. The past two years had weathered him into a seasoned professional. His mouth formed a firm, serious line. His head was cocked, eyes and ears attentive. The firm, taut muscles of his hard biceps glistened in the dim glow from the Edison bulb over the sink.

His fingers moved with nimble, expert ease. The sight of his sidearm sent a chill up her spine. Savannah was no stranger to handguns. She'd grown up in Texas, where firearms were ubiquitous. Matt had taken her to the firing range when they were dating, insisting she learn how to shoot.

She recalled how it felt to pull the trigger. The kick. The smoke. The acrid smell. And unexpectedly, a sense of power. Exhilarating almost. Watching him now with the cold steel in his hands, that pucker of a scar on his right upper arm where he'd been shot, brought back dark memories.

She closed her eyes and tried to fight off the barrage of images that floated through her mind, to no avail. The fight in the bar. A flash of metal in the dim light. Jackie Spencer's screams. A beer bottle shattering on the concrete floor.

And then the gun blast.

A deafening noise in the confines of the bar. A sound she would never forget. Nor could she forget the startled look of surprise on Matt's face as he staggered back and dropped to his knees, blood blossoming down the sleeve of his shirt.

"Savannah?"

Matt's voice broke through to her. She opened her eyes, felt a tear slip down her cheek.

"Honey? Are you all right?"

She shook her head.

"You want to talk about it?"

"I'm okay." She swiped away the tear.

"You were thinking about the time I got shot?"

Even after all these years, the man still knew her so well. He saw through her like a pane of glass. She swallowed a lump in her throat and pressed the back of her hand against her nose. "Yes."

Matt laid the gun down on the red-and-white-checkered fabric tablecloth, pushed his chair back, and opened his arms to her. "Come here."

And she went to him, like a lost child seeking protection.

She knelt on the floor in front of him, but he pulled her into his lap and pressed her head to his chest. She hadn't meant to cry, but the avalanche of tears refused to be dammed up any longer. She sobbed in huge, shuddering gulps. They'd both lost so much.

"Shh," Matt soothed. "It's okay. I won't let them hurt you."

Her fingers curled against his chest, fisting a handful of T-shirt. She wanted to tell him it wasn't her safety she feared for, but his own.

He rocked her back and forth as gently as she might rock Cody. He pressed his lips to her ear and murmured words of reassurance. She breathed in his masculine smell—

leather, oil, gunpowder. It stirred something primordial within her.

Matt hugged her closer, resting his cheek on the top of her head, and she absorbed his essence, taking comfort from his strength.

"I've missed you so much," he breathed, threading his fingers through her hair. "You can't imagine how many nights I've lain awake thinking about you, about this, about what used to be."

Savannah knew she should draw away, put a stop to the fantasy he was spinning, but she couldn't. Her arms refused to let go. Her legs wouldn't obey. For now, she needed the sheltering security of his arms.

He hooked a callused index finger under her chin and forced her to look at him. "I want you," he said simply.

Her heart galloped like a herd of stampeding cattle, beating thunderously against her chest.

Gently, he tightened his grip on her. His thigh muscles knotted rock hard beneath her bottom. She nestled her head against his shoulder, lacing her arms around his neck.

He angled his head and kissed her forehead—sweetly, tenderly. Kissed her eyelids, the tip of her nose, the delicate groove between her nose and mouth.

He stopped at her lips and waited.

She looked at him.

"More?" he asked.

She nodded. "More."

His lips touched hers. Soft. Smooth. Malleable. Moving his head, he traced her lips with his fingers, his touch featherfine. He quirked an eyebrow at her and smiled knowingly. "You sure you want more?"

"Please."

"Remember, sweetheart, you asked for this."

And she would have to deal with the consequences later—

but for now, she simply floated, allowing herself to be enveloped by his essence, her heart beating in perfect harmony with his.

His mouth returned to hers, this time not so benignly. Innocence became knowledge as he captured her bottom lip between his teeth, and he growled, low and raspy.

A wave of love crested through her. Pure physical need swelled inside her. Greedily, she drank from his lips, savoring the taste that was uniquely Matt Forrester.

The kiss elongated, stretching into forever. Man with woman. Soft against hard. Pressure building, climbing, escalating. Savannah pressed her body into his and let herself go free.

Moaning, he upped the tempo, urging her lips to part and accept his searching tongue.

She accepted him. Accepted her own hunger. Accepted the moment for what it was. Pleasure. Luxury. Indulgence. She asked for nothing beyond this instant, knowing that more might not be possible.

Briefly, he pulled his mouth away, leaving her bereft.

"Oh, Savannah." He whispered her name like a litany, a prayer he revered every night. "You torture me so."

It wasn't her intention to torment him, but she understood the double-edged blade because it lashed her, too. She wanted him so badly, yet if she allowed herself to give in to him completely, she knew she would lose all common sense.

Only two things in her life had hurt more than breaking up with Matt. Her father's desertion and her mother's death.

If her mother had lived, she might not have panicked and married Gary as a way to care for herself and Ginger. If she'd had time to reason, had not been so immersed in grief, she might have made a different decision. But she'd been young and frightened and alone in the world except for the younger sister who'd depended on her.

Matt stroked her hair. His breath warmed her cheek. Right here, right now, she felt protected. But she knew only too well that feeling of safety was false. One single crack from a gun, one bullet, and that security could shatter forever.

"I came on too strong, didn't I?" he whispered.

"We can't pick up where we left off," she answered. "We're not the same people we were back then."

"No," he agreed. "We're not."

The bond between them flowed much deeper now. It extended beyond the external pleasures of the flesh, encompassed more than fleeting moments of fun, and that frightened Savannah. Instead of dissipating with time and distance, their feelings for each other had developed and grown into something more mature.

If she could make love with Matt and then just walk away, she would do it in a twinkling. But she was not capable of that. Her feelings for Matt ran too deep. If she ever made love to him again, Savannah knew the man would possess her, mind, body, and soul. And she didn't know if she was ready for that.

To save them both from rash action, she took a deep breath and wriggled off his lap.

"It's past my bedtime," she said, her voice wobbling.

He nodded as if he understood all the thoughts sprinting through her brain.

"Yeah," he said, his own voice none too steady. "You need your rest."

She stared down at her hands, unable to meet his gaze. "I'll get blankets and pillows for the couch."

He picked up his gun and started reassembling it. She noticed his fingers trembled ever so slightly. "Don't worry, Savvy, I'll protect you."

"I know you will, Matt. It's what you do best."

She moved past him, but he reached out and snagged her

arm. She looked down at him, her thoughts chasing each other like kids playing tag under the streetlamps.

"What happens once Larkins and Thompson are in jail?"

She looked into his eyes and said the truest thing she knew. "I don't know, Matt. I honestly don't know."

14

The grandfather clock emitted one resounding bong. Matt had flip-flopped on the couch for hours, his feet hanging off the end, his mind spinning in a random pattern, his blood surging through his body, thick and hot.

He couldn't stop thinking about Savannah.

Her cool vanilla scent rose up from the linens, wrapping him in a cocoon of bittersweet nostalgia. Her soft, pliant lips haunted his memory. His arms ached to hold her.

She slept just yards away. Down the hall. Only a thin wooden door separated them.

He fought visions of himself kicking down that door, hollering her name. Insisting that they were meant to be together. He saw himself gathering her to his chest and making love to her throughout the night. Convincing her once and for all that they could end their miserable loneliness lost in each other's arms.

Matt blew out a slow, deep breath. *Think of Larkins and Thompson*, a voice in the back of his head insisted. The same workaholic voice that had driven him to succeed these past two years. The voice that had kept him sane when Savannah married Gary.

It still stung, although now he understood her motivation better. She'd been a pregnant, scared, twenty-three-year-old, a dying mother and younger sister to support. And he'd been no help at all, getting shot in a bar fight, then disappearing on her to attend specialized training and a job in El Paso. He hated not knowing about the misunderstanding when she'd come to his house and saw him with Jackie. Matt winced at the memory. That must have hurt her almost as badly as her marriage to Gary had hurt him.

Marrying Gary to provide for her little sister and Matt's unborn son had probably cost Savannah more than he would ever know. She'd swallowed her pride, put her feelings for him aside, and proceeded to do what had to be done to survive. How could he blame her for that?

Suddenly, Matt felt like the world's biggest jerk. He'd behaved like a spoiled brat, blaming Savannah for leaving him, when in reality, he was the one who had abandoned her. Just like her father had abandoned her those many years ago.

She'd been young, alone, desperate. And she had turned to the only man who'd offered a helping hand. Markum had been there for her, while he'd been off chasing his own dreams. Hot shame flooded Matt's body.

Markum had offered her a home, financial support, and a name for her baby. She'd jumped at the chance.

In the wake of the news of her marriage, after his completion of specialized detective training, he'd accepted a job with a police department in El Paso. It had given him the opportunity to learn and concentrate on his career. But deep in his heart, he'd always known he would return home to Rascal.

If he admitted the truth to himself, he confessed that news of Markum's death had given him hope for a second chance.

But was it too late to make amends? Too late to start anew? Matt's eyelids drooped. He'd had precious little sleep over the last few days. Exhaustion had almost claimed him when the creak of a floorboard jerked him awake. Disoriented for a moment, he lurched to a sitting position, his blanket sliding to the floor.

Another creak.

Matt reached for the handgun underneath his pillow and squinted into the darkness, every muscle tense, alert. Two years working for a large metropolitan police force had sharpened his instincts.

Savannah drifted down the hallway, a pale, shimmering ghost in her white cotton nightgown.

"Savannah?" he croaked as he placed his duty weapon on the coffee table and got to his feet.

Had she come to him after all? Had she decided she wanted him as much as he wanted her? The possibility sent a rapturous shudder coursing down his spine.

She didn't answer him, didn't move.

"Savvy?"

She floated across the floor. Her eyes stared straight ahead, unseeing.

"Mama?" she whispered. "Is that you?"

That single word cleaved a hole through Matt's heart. He realized with a start that Savannah was sleepwalking. He reached for her.

She collapsed against his chest.

"It's okay, sweetheart," he soothed, pressing his cheek against the top of her head and whispering into her hair.

She whimpered, eyes still unfocused. Did she sleepwalk often? He didn't want to awaken her. Best she remained asleep and blissfully ignorant.

He sank down on the couch, drawing her with him. Wrapping himself around her trembling frame. He tucked her into the curve of his arms, and they lay like spoons, nestled side by side on the couch.

A perfect fit.

If only he could hold her like this for eternity. Burrowing his face in the back of her neck, he pressed his lips to her velvety skin and inhaled her delicious aroma. Her sweet vanilla scent brought to mind rich, chewy, chocolate chip cookies, softly flickering candles, and warm, sudsy bubble baths.

Memories rolled through his mind.

Savannah, fresh from a swim at Turner Falls, a skimpy, pink-and-green swimsuit clinging to her curves, looking for the world like an exotic sea goddess.

Savannah, on their first date, the shy coquette, who'd turned quickly playful, suddenly ready to surrender herself to him, until he'd been the one to apply the brakes before things had gotten out of control.

Savannah, indignant over having her cattle stolen, her lovely features creasing into a frown as she wondered how she would pay the bills and continue to support her little family.

Savannah, on Ginger's wedding day, proud surrogate mother, smiling majestically, head held high, shoulders straight, watching as he gave away the sister she'd ushered into adulthood.

And Savannah, the fierce Madonna, sitting at her kitchen table, cradling Cody to her chest, her face glowing with love for their son.

Ah, hell, Matt thought and gulped past the lump in his throat. *How stupid could one hardheaded man be?*

SAVANNAH OPENED HER EYES.

A predawn glow blushed through the half-drawn drapes,

slanting a rosy shadow across the room. Blinking, she stared at the coffee table and saw Matt's gun resting there. She frowned. What on earth?

Her gaze traveled downward. Burly forearms bunched around her midsection. Hissing in a breath, Savannah realized she was lying on the living room couch encircled by Matt's embrace.

His chin pressed into her upper back, his pelvis molded against her hips, and his hairy legs entwined with hers. Faint snoring rumbled near her ear.

Oh my gosh. She panicked, her thoughts conjuring wild scenarios. *How did I get here? What happened last night? Have I been sleepwalking again?* It was an affliction that had plagued her on several occasions after her mother's death, but she hadn't sleepwalked since Cody's birth, and never with such disastrous consequences.

Gingerly, she lifted Matt's right arm and tried to slide from his grasp. He mumbled incoherently, snuggled deeper, and clung tighter.

Oh dear, oh dear. How to extricate herself without waking him?

She tried again, easing her left leg to the floor. Her toes curled into the rug. One limb freed.

Shifting, she tried to scoot her buttocks away from him, but he only pulled her closer and tunneled a hand underneath the hem of her nightshirt.

Savannah froze.

Matt's palm was grafted to her upper thigh. Was he awake, feigning sleep, and enjoying her plight? He wouldn't do that. Would he?

"Matt," she whispered, trying to ignore the warm sensations radiating from his hand throughout her leg and beyond.

No response.

She waited, listening.

His chest rose and fell against her back in a slow, steady rhythm. Dead asleep. Some protector he turned out to be. This guy would have slept through a tornado. The thieves could have waltzed in and stolen the clothing off their bodies without him being any the wiser.

Savannah lay there a moment, one leg on the floor, the other captured beneath Matt's weight, straddling the edge of the couch and contemplating her next move. Briefly, she considered elbowing him in the ribs. She smiled. That plan of action held some appeal. She might have been sleepwalking, but he was the one who'd allowed her to curl up next to him.

From the bedroom, she heard Cody whimper.

To heck with this. Abruptly, she shoved Matt's arm aside.

His snore turned into a snort. Bolting upright, Matt dumped Savannah to the floor in a tangled sprawl. He scrambled to his feet and fumbled for his gun on the coffee table.

"What's happened? What's going on? Are Larkins and Thompson after the cattle?" he shouted.

Savannah stared up at him. His eyes were bleary. His dark hair stuck out at various angles. Pillow creases lined his face. Pale legs protruded from his bright-red boxer shorts, contrasting markedly with his tanned bare chest and arms.

Savannah burst into peals of laughter.

"What's so funny?" he growled.

"Where's my cell phone? I need a picture of this," she managed past the fit of giggles. "I could blackmail you with threats of posting this on social media."

Chuffing, Matt located his leather holster thrown over the back of the couch and holstered the weapon. He retrieved his undershirt from the floor and tugged it over his head. Helplessly, Savannah's gaze followed his every move. Matt was one fine specimen of manhood.

"Quit staring at me." He ran a hand through his hair to

tame his mussed locks. "I must look like the back end of a bull."

"About as friendly as one, too. I'd forgotten how grouchy you are in the mornings," she teased.

"Hmph."

She extended her hand. "Help me up, and I'll go put on the coffee."

He reached down to boost her to her feet. Their hands touched. The sexual gleam in his eyes had Savannah sucking in a deep breath.

They both seemed to realize the amorous nature of their situation at the same time. Two semi-naked adults who'd spent the night wrapped in each other's arms on the edge of a couch. Savannah quickly averted her gaze.

Matt faked a cough.

Cody's wail broke the tension.

They started for the bedroom at the same time and collided into each other. Savannah's head caught Matt on the chin.

"Ouch," he complained, stroking his jaw.

"Didn't help me much, either." She massaged the top of her head with a hand.

"I'll go get the baby, you put on the coffee," he said.

"I'm sure he's wet. Unless you want to change a diaper, you better put on the coffee, and I'll get Cody."

"Okay."

She went to the bedroom. Matt headed for the kitchen.

Savannah turned on the light and greeted her son with a tender smile. "Morning, Cody Coo, are you hungry?"

He quieted instantly and reached for her with both arms outstretched.

"Bet my big boy is wet, too." She changed his diaper, then lifted him over the crib railing. She was always amazed at how light he felt in the mornings. He clutched her neck, pressing slobbery kisses to her cheek.

Savannah laughed. Joy bubbled inside her as she waltzed Cody into the kitchen. Her heart floated free and as giddy as a kid's kite in March. Her son never failed to cheer her. And she was so relieved to have told Matt about Cody being his son. It had lifted a huge burden off her shoulders.

But they still needed to talk about what this meant for their future. Child support. Visitation rights. She and Matt were inextricably tied together for life. Their son was the unbreakable common thread.

Matt had not only started the coffee, but he'd also set a skillet of bacon on to cook. He stood at the stove, tongs in his hand. Bread in the toaster. While she'd changed Cody, Matt had shimmied into his blue jeans and plaid cotton shirt.

Feeling conspicuous in her nightgown, Savannah settled Cody into his high chair, then went back to her bedroom to dress in work clothes. She returned to find Matt talking to Cody and peeling a banana for him.

Was this what it would have been like to be married to Matt, she wondered, a stab of loss needling her. The two of them, cooking breakfast together, and sharing parenting duties?

"Hi, Mommy," Matt said, his gaze roving over her body.

Savannah didn't miss the look of appreciation reflected in his eyes. She felt a heated flush run the length of her neck. To distract herself, she reached into the cabinet and grabbed two coffee mugs. Pouring the coffee, she remembered Matt took his black. She slid the mug across the counter to him, then leveled two spoonfuls of sugar into her own cup.

Cody garbled in a singsong voice "da-da, da-da," and smashed handfuls of banana against the high chair tray.

Savannah leaned against the counter and sipped her coffee. The scene before her looked so natural, so domestic.

A nugget of longing caught in her throat, and she wished she could hold on to this moment forever.

❧

"YOU LIKE YOUR EGGS SUNNY-SIDE UP, RIGHT?" MATT cracked two eggs into the frying pan. Why couldn't he stop grinning? He just kept smiling and smiling and smiling. Was this what it would feel like to wake up beside Savannah every morning? To wake up to family life?

"You remembered how I like my eggs." She sounded touched.

"I remember most everything about you, Savvy," he whispered. His tongue stiffened against his teeth. He heaved in a breath, searching for the inner strength to continue. His chest muscles bunched, tight and knotted. "Your scent haunts me. It's so genuine. So simple. Like bright sunshine and homemade bread."

Matt set down the tongs and stepped halfway across the kitchen in one stride. He placed both hands on her shoulders, gazing directly into her eyes. "The way you move," he continued. "So refined and graceful."

She fluttered those sandy eyelashes at him, then set her coffee cup on the counter.

His blood pressure climbed a notch as he continued. "I remember how ticklish you are in that one spot right behind your knees and..."

"Okay," she said sharply. She placed her palms on his chest and pushed him away. "I get the picture."

Defense mechanism, he thought. She was trying to guard her feelings, hide behind apathy, but he wouldn't let her. Not now. Not this time.

He winked broadly and picked up a spatula to flip the

eggs. "Yeah. You're right. That memory is definitely X-rated. Better not mention it in front of our baby."

"You're outrageous."

"Oh yeah?"

"Yes."

She wanted outrageous? He'd give her outrageous. Before she could protest or discourage him, he drew her into his arms.

They gazed at each other, spellbound, both too terrified to hope.

He cupped her chin in his hand and wrapped his other arm around her waist. His touch was light, hesitant, searching.

Savannah gulped, her lips parted.

He lowered his head.

She caught her breath.

And then he kissed her. Long, hot, and searing.

A knock at the back entrance startled them both. Savannah jumped away and rubbed the back of her hand against her mouth.

Matt stalked to the door and threw it open.

Clem walked in. "Am I interrupting something?"

Matt pulled out a chair and waved Clem into it. Savannah poured a cup of coffee for the elderly man. Matt plated the food, turned off the burners. Offered Clem breakfast.

"What happened with Larkins and Thompson?" he asked.

"Didn't even find them until after midnight." Clem tucked into the eggs with gusto. "And by then, they'd already been through a fifth of whiskey. They were too drunk to talk sense to."

Matt nodded. "I suspected as much."

"If you knew that, why did you stay here last night?" Savannah asked.

Not answering her, Matt sat down beside Clem. "Tell me everything."

"I told 'em you arrested Miss Savannah last night, that the farmhouse was sitting wide open, and that you'd brought six Gerts back home."

"Did they seem interested?" Matt leaned forward, the muscles in his arms bunching as he tensed.

"They'll be back," Clem predicted.

Yes! Matt had the criminals right where he wanted them. "I've got to go into the office for a few hours, Savannah. I want you and Cody to come with me."

"And do what? Sit around a police station with a fifteen-month-old? I don't think so."

"I'll drop you off at my apartment."

She shook her head. "We'll be fine. What could Thompson and Larkins possibly do in broad daylight?"

Matt sighed. "Savvy, you make my job too tough."

"There's no reason to uproot Cody from his routine."

"All right. If you're going to stay here, I'll get Sheriff Langley to post a deputy outside in a car to watch the house until I get back. End of discussion."

She saluted him. "Anything else, Your Lordship?"

Matt grinned. "Lordship. I like that."

She stuck her tongue out at him. "You would."

"I'm serious, Savannah. Larkins and Thompson can be dangerous, especially if they've been drinking. Stay in the house, don't go to the door, or take any phone calls. Got it?"

"All right."

"If someone unfamiliar shows up, I want you to text me right away."

"Okay."

Matt resisted the urge to bend down and kiss her again. Her lips beckoned to him, full, dewy, waiting to be plucked like a ripe peach. If Clem hadn't interrupted when he had...

well, they might be rolling on the floor this very minute, clutched in a wild embrace.

"Lock this door after we leave," he said, wishing he didn't have to go. Wishing he had time to eat breakfast with her.

Savannah rolled her eyes. "All *right.*"

He located his Stetson in the living room and plunked it on his head. "Clem's going to be on the lookout until the deputy arrives."

"Stop nagging, Forrester, I get the picture."

"I just don't want you pulling some hardheaded stunt."

"I won't. I promise."

If anything happens to her or the boy, I'll never forgive myself. "I'll be back long before noon."

"Not if you don't ever get out the door."

"Lock up," he admonished. Lord, how he wanted to kiss her again.

Savannah gripped Cody's hand. "Tell Daddy bye-bye."

Daddy. What a beautiful word.

"Bye!" Cody squealed suddenly. "Da-da."

Savannah smiled at Matt. The sight drove a stab of longing clean through Matt's guts. He was going to do everything in his power for a second chance with her. Cody deserved to have his father in his life. They deserved to be a family.

SAVANNAH FELT DOWNRIGHT CLAUSTROPHOBIC. CODY WAS napping, and she had nothing to do after she ate the breakfast Matt made her. Picking up the remote control, she flipped through the television channels. Nothing caught her interest.

Sighing, she turned off the TV. Never one to stay indoors for long, she hated being cooped up inside. It drove her crazy. She wanted to go out and dig in her garden or help Clem with chores. If only Ginger were around to talk to, but she was on her honeymoon.

Joe Greely, the deputy from Sheriff Langley's office that had driven her home, arrived around eight-thirty, not long after Matt left the Circle B, and parked his patrol car behind the barn so that it wasn't immediately visible from the road.

Picking up a book, she stared at the words, unable to concentrate. She put it down. Paced. She'd already cleaned the house. Maybe she'd give herself a pedicure.

Her landline rang. Cell reception was spotty in the Davis Mountains, making a landline a necessity. Yay. Something to do. She reached for the phone but then hesitated. Matt had warned her not to answer it.

The phone rang again.

Savannah glanced at the caller ID. Unknown caller.

Had Larkins or Thompson somehow gotten her landline number? Were they calling to check up on Clem's story, to see if anyone was home?

The third ring echoed throughout the living room and sent a tingle of apprehension sliding down her spine. What if it was something important?

She closed her eyes on the fourth ring, her fingers fairly itching to answer.

Fifth ring.

Why didn't they hang up?

Sixth ring.

What if it was Matt?

Seventh ring.

Something had to be wrong. Savannah took a deep breath. What could it hurt to answer? If it was an unfamiliar voice, she could pretend they had the wrong number. Tentatively, she raised the cordless phone to her ear.

"Hello?"

"Sa...Savannah?" A woman's voice.

Someone was crying. "Yes?"

"Vannah... it's me, Ginger."

Dread tore through her heart in a white-hot second. "Ginger? Honey? What's wrong? Where are you?"

"I'm at the bus station."

"In Rascal?"

"Uh-huh."

"But you're supposed to be in Cancun. What happened?"

"I came home." Her sister sniffled into the phone.

"Is Todd with you?" Savannah asked.

Silence.

"Gin? You still there?"

"I left him, Vannah. My marriage is over."

"Oh, honey." Savannah didn't know what to say. She sank down into a chair, resting her forehead in her palm.

"Can you come get me, sis? Please? I need to come home."

15

Savannah hung up the phone, her thoughts spinning like the tilt-a-whirl at the county fair. What to do? She couldn't leave her sister stranded at the bus station, and besides, she was dying to know what had happened between Ginger and Todd.

But Matt had warned her not to leave the ranch, and she didn't want to put Cody in danger. Conflicted, Savannah ran a hand through her hair and sighed.

It would take less than an hour to drive to Rascal, pick up Ginger, and return to the Circle B. No big deal. She'd tell Deputy Joe Greely where she was going, and he could follow her if he wanted to. Or heck, he could even go get Ginger for her.

"Bye!" Cody sang out. He patted his chubby palms and grinned. "Bye Da-da! Bye cows."

"Aunt Ginger's gonna be surprised by you," Savannah told him. "Learning new words."

"Bye!"

"Yes, we're going bye-bye to pick up Aunt Ginger."

Savannah gnawed her bottom lip, wondering what Todd had done. If he'd laid one hand on her sister, she'd strangle him.

Picking Cody up, Savannah went outside to talk to the deputy. She cornered the barn. His patrol car was empty.

"Joe? You there?" She paused. Not wanting to bother him if he'd gone to relieve himself. "Are you there? It's me, Savannah."

No reply.

She glanced around. There was no sign of Joe.

Shoot. No doubt Joe was off observing the call of nature.

She didn't have time to wait for him. The sooner she went into town, the sooner they'd get back. She debated about leaving him a note, then decided against it. What if, by some wide stretch of the imagination, Larkins and Thompson did happen by and found the note? No. Better to go after Ginger and get right home.

And Matt would have a fit when he found out she'd disobeyed him.

Okay, she'd text Matt and let him know what was going on. She went to her car, buckled Cody into his car seat, got out her phone, and sent Matt a text.

Ginger left Todd. Picking her up @ the bus station.

She waited for his response.

She noticed that her message hadn't been delivered. Crummy cell reception. She'd try again when she got on the other side of the mountain.

Cody fell asleep almost immediately. It seemed an eternity passed before she arrived at the bus station in Rascal. Parked beside a curb meter. Savannah released Cody from his car seat and carried him inside the bus station with her, her gaze sweeping the small crowd moving through the building. It was only then that she realized she'd forgotten to text Matt again. Oh well, she was already here.

"Do you see Aunt Ginger?" she asked Cody.

"Bye!"

Savannah craned her neck, finally spotting her sister sitting on her suitcase off to one side. Ginger, looking pale despite her tan, held a tissue to her red-rimmed eyes, her shoulders hunched to her ears.

"Ginger." Savannah waved a hand and slipped around the people.

"Vannah." Ginger bolted to her feet and raced over to throw her arms around Savannah and Cody.

"Oh, honey. I'm so sorry."

"I made such a m...m...mistake." Ginger hiccupped. "Just like you did with Gary."

"No," Savannah said sharply. "Don't say that."

Ginger's words grated against her heart, rough as sandpaper. Ginger and Todd had been so in love. Whatever problems her sister faced in her marriage, it did not mirror Savannah's own blunder. Her mistake had been in not marrying the man *she* loved.

Savannah reached over and tucked a strand of strawberry blond hair behind Ginger's ear. "Let's get you home."

She grabbed Ginger's carry-on bag, while her sister collected the bigger suitcase. They didn't speak again until they were in the car, headed to the ranch.

"So tell me, what went wrong?" Savannah asked.

"We didn't fight, exactly." Ginger blew her nose.

"Oh?"

"In fact, Todd doesn't even know I flew home."

"What? You didn't even tell him you were leaving?"

"He probably hasn't even noticed I'm gone," Ginger wailed. "It was supposed to be our honeymoon, but all he did was work."

"What?"

"That's right." Ginger nodded. "He offered insurance advice to everyone we met. One guy was interested in a policy, and the next thing I knew, they were playing golf together, and Todd had forgotten all about me."

"I'm sure he didn't forget you. Todd loves his job, and he's such a hardworking man. I bet he was just thinking how much he wanted to provide for you."

"I married a workaholic," Ginger wailed.

"Do you think you might have overreacted?"

Ginger glared. "Whose side are you on?"

"I'm not taking sides, sweetie." She reached over and patted her sister's shoulder. "I just hate to see you end your marriage without thinking long and hard about the consequences. Maybe give Todd the benefit of the doubt."

Ginger burst into a fresh round of tears. "Last night, I got all dressed up for dinner in a sexy new dress, and Todd ended up falling asleep! On our honeymoon."

"Maybe he was tired."

"Or bored." She sobbed. "I guess I'm not as interesting as business meetings and insurance deals."

Savannah shook her head. "Did you at least tell him how you were feeling? Give him a chance to explain?"

Ginger's chin quivered. "No. I packed my bags, and I left. Let him figure out why."

"Did you leave a note? Anything?"

She shook her head.

"Ginger!" Savannah gasped. "You will call Todd the minute we get home. I imagine he's out of his mind with worry. Probably has the whole of Cancun out looking for you."

"I bet he hasn't even noticed I'm gone," she said petulantly.

"You *will* call him, Ginger Renee Prentiss Baxter! Or I will."

Ginger hunkered down in her seat. "He made me feel so insignificant."

"The same Todd who couldn't keep his hands off you just a week ago? I can't hardly believe that."

"Marriage changed him," Ginger said gloomily.

Savannah pulled into the driveway and killed the engine. Cody had fallen asleep again on the way home, his little head slumped sideways in the car seat. Savannah glanced at her watch. She'd been gone exactly an hour.

Opening the car door, Savannah experienced an odd sensation, as if they were being watched. The hairs on the back of her neck prickled.

The ranch lay strangely silent. No mooing cattle, no singing birds. Perhaps she should go check on Joe.

"I'll carry Cody," Ginger volunteered, reaching over to unbuckle the baby.

"Let's hurry and get into the house," Savannah told her sister, sneaking glances around the perimeter. Nothing looked out of place, and yet, she couldn't shake the creepy sensation trailing down her spine.

"Why?" Ginger asked.

"I'll explain later. Hurry." Savannah draped an arm across her sister's shoulders, ushering her toward the house.

For the first time since Matt had left, fear snaked through her. He'd said Larkins and Thompson could be dangerous. Especially if they'd been drinking. Were the drunken thieves lying in wait for them at this very moment? The idea sent a shudder through her body. Matt had told her that both men had served time in Huntsville.

Savannah gnawed her bottom lip. She was probably worrying needlessly, letting her imagination run away with her. But she couldn't shake the disturbing feeling that someone *was* watching them.

They reached the back door, and Savannah fumbled in her purse for the keys while Ginger stood to one side, holding Cody.

Her hands trembled. The key slipped. Grated against the metal. *Calm down*. She was freaking herself out.

"Um... Vannah." The tone of Ginger's voice struck panic in Savannah's heart.

She turned her head to look at her sister.

Ginger was pointing at something.

Her gaze leaped to where she pointed. There, near the open barn door, lying face down in the dirt, was Clem. His frail body terrifyingly still, blood caked at his temple, a shattered whiskey bottle near his head.

Savannah's breath evaporated. Her knees wobbled. Her mouth went dry. A stitch snagged her lower abdomen. The keys dropped from her hand and jangled, unnoticed, to the porch.

"Vannah," Ginger whispered, "is Clem dead?"

❧

MATT FORRESTER STROLLED INTO KELLY'S BAR, WHIPPED off his Stetson, and perched on a bar stool.

"How are you doing, Jackie?" Matt asked the curvaceous blonde behind the counter. He threaded fingers through his hair to tame it into place. "I didn't know you were back in Rascal."

"Hey, cowboy." Jackie grinned. "Long time no see. The big city wasn't for me. I'm a small-town girl."

"I hear that. I'm back home for good, too."

"Well, I've heard there's cattle rustling going on over at the Circle B."

"Gossip sure gets around."

"That's Rascal for you." Her gaze traveled the length of him, a sexual gleam sparking in her eye. "So tell me, are you and Savannah rekindling your relationship? Or are you a free man?"

Matt was damned glad the bar was almost vacant. "Savannah is the only woman for me."

Jackie fished an olive out of a jar with a green plastic cocktail sword. Placing her elbow on the bar, she slid her upper body forward until she and Matt were eye to eye. Languidly, she pushed the olive into her mouth, pulled the sword through her teeth, then laughed low and husky. "Sorry to hear it."

"You're a naughty one, Jackie Spencer." He shook his head ruefully.

She sighed, then straightened. "Can't blame a girl for trying."

"Actually, I came in to see if you'd seen hide or hair of Brent Larkins and Hootie Thompson the last few days. I got a bad feeling those two have been up to no good."

"Sure. They were in here this morning." She swiped a towel across the bar.

Matt frowned. "You didn't happen to hear what they were discussing, did you?"

Jackie flipped a strand of hair over her shoulder. "Yeah. That old ranch hand from the Circle B. What's his name? Clyde. No, Clem."

"What'd they say?"

"They were cussin', raising a ruckus. Said the old man owed 'em more gambling money. Kept bragging about how they were going to collect."

"What time did they leave?"

She leaned against the counter. "An hour and a half ago, when they ran out of money."

Matt tensed. He didn't like the sound of this. "You wouldn't happen to know where they were headed?"

"Said they were going to the Circle B to get their money from Clem one way or the other."

Matt bounded off the stool so fast it spun. Grabbing his

Stetson, he headed for the door, his hand automatically reaching to pat the sidearm hidden beneath his jacket.

"Matt? Is something up?"

"Pray I'm wrong, Jackie. I think Savannah might be in a heap of trouble."

The heavy wooden door slammed behind him. Matt stalked across the parking lot as fast as his legs would take him. He'd meant to set a fire under those two punks, but he hadn't expected them to converge on the Circle B in broad daylight. Mentally cursing himself for his stupidity, he jumped into his Jeep and keyed the starter.

Sweat dripped down his brow. He bumped onto the road, rolled down the window, slapped the portable siren to the hood, and punched the accelerator.

The Circle B lay twenty miles away. Matt felt as if it were two thousand.

"Calm down, Forrester," he told himself. "You're probably overreacting."

But his gut crunched up like a coiled spring. Something was wrong. He knew it. And it was all his fault. He shouldn't have left Savannah alone. Should have insisted she stay at his apartment despite her protests.

He grasped the police band radio speaker in one hand and tried to raise Joe Greely. Nothing but static. He tried again, then waited.

Still no reply.

Damn. Where was Joe?

"Please let her be okay," Matt prayed. His plan had detonated in his face. If anything happened to Savannah, he knew he could never forgive himself.

A lifetime passed before he turned onto the dirt road that led to the Circle B. Matt jammed his boot to the floor. The Jeep hurtled forward, spewing dirt and gravel. Only another mile. The tires chewed the road as Matt raced up the hill.

"Please," he prayed again. "Please, let me be in time."

❧

"Is he alive?" Ginger breathed. Cody clutched in her arms.

Savannah squatted over Clem's body, her fingers searching his wrist for a pulse. At first, she felt nothing. Panic released adrenaline. Her own pulse skittered erratically. She kept trying.

Wait. Was that a beat? Yes. Thready but definitely there.

"He's alive," she said, relief shooting through her body. Her shoulders sagged, and she rocked back on her heels.

"Oh, thank God."

"Ginger, take Cody into the house. Call 911 and get an ambulance out here. Then call Matt."

Ginger stood gawking, her eyes round as plates.

"Move!"

Jerked from her trance, Ginger sprinted across the yard, found the keys on the porch, and let herself into the house. Savannah returned her attention to Clem. His color was ashen, the wasted gray of mottling clay, and his hands were so cold.

Think. Savannah chewed her lip. She'd taken a first aid class when her mother was sick. What did she remember?

How bad was the laceration? Her fingers probed his hairline. Blood, viscous and dark, trickled from the gash on his scalp. Deep but not life-threatening.

Savannah sucked in air. What kind of low-life scum would do this to a helpless old man? She gritted her teeth, wanting to throw back her head and scream out her rage. But she could not afford to give in to anger. She must keep calm.

Clem was probably in shock. He had to be kept warm. She needed blankets.

There were horse blankets in the tack room. It was closer than the house, and she'd still be able to keep Clem in view.

Getting to her feet, she stumbled, feeling a bit dizzy as the blood rushed to her head. She put a hand on the side of the barn to steady herself.

Thump.

What was that? Savannah frowned. Had the noise come from inside the barn? She kicked the door open wider with the toe of her boot. Adrenaline surged through her system. Was Clem's assailant still inside the building?

"Who's there?" she demanded, trying to sound brave. A sudden chill ran through her. What if the criminals were hiding in the barn?

She stood, poised for flight, her thoughts racing. Should she go after a blanket? Try to drag Clem into the house? No. She remembered being warned against moving an accident victim. Squaring her shoulders, she made her decision. Clem needed her help; this was no time for cowardice. Resolutely, Savannah stepped into the barn.

The odor of oats and hay clung in the air, heavy and overpowering. Narrowing her eyes, Savannah darted a quick glance around the cluttered room. Straw lay strewn over the floor. Gardening equipment rested against one wall in haphazard order. Dust motes rode a shaft of sunlight sloping through the small, grimy window overhead.

She stepped forward. Stopped. Waited. Listened.

Silence.

Don't be such a scaredy-cat.

Savannah drew in a deep breath and moved into the tack room. Keeping her legs stiff to bolster her courage, she grabbed for a horse blanket thrown over the rack.

Creak.

She froze, the coarse blanket clutched in her outstretched

hands. Jerking her head toward the open door, she saw a shadow fall across the floor.

Fear catapulted bile into her throat. Goosebumps spread over her skin like a rash. Her heart constricted. Before she could run, before she could scream, a sweaty hand was clamped over her mouth.

Instinct begged her to bite, to fight, to get away. She opened her mouth, intending to chomp down on the pad of the stranger's palm when she heard the ominous click of a cocked gun and felt cold metal pressed to her temple.

"Better not try it, sister, unless you want to leave a motherless child behind," a gravelly voice lashed out.

Terror iced her guts, slick as frozen cement. A wiry arm snaked around her waist, pulling her tight against the trespasser's body.

Savannah's five senses stood at attention. Her nostrils quivered. She smelled the strong odor of dirt, mold, and sweat. Fear branded her tongue—brackish, salty, bitter.

Blood roared in her ears, as loud as a tornado. A fly buzzed at the window, the sound amplified, expanded, until her head was filled with the strumming noise. Her heart hammered like a long-distance runner. She felt the intruder's rude arm tighten around her waist.

Her vision sharpened. She viewed every aspect of the barn in vivid detail—the jagged crack running along the wall, a coil of rope nestled in the corner beside one stall, a pair of old work gloves knotted on a shelf next to a jar of nails.

Shifting her eyes, she could see Clem's dormant body through the open door, stretched out on the ground.

"Yeah," the ugly voice behind her said. "Your handyman got in the way. That stupid deputy sheriff, too. Thought he could fool me by hiding his patrol car behind the barn. Maybe they're both dead, maybe they ain't. I don't rightly care."

Savannah's heart sank. She could expect no help from Deputy Joe.

"You're in something of a fix, sister."

Where was the other thief? Matt had said there were two. What if the other outlaw had somehow gotten to Ginger and Cody? The thought drove spikes of terror through her lungs.

Please, God, let Ginger stay locked in the house. Let them be okay.

"Now, I'm gonna let go of your mouth, but don't you scream, or the gun goes off. And I want you to keep facing forward, don't look at me. Get my drift?"

Savannah nodded. Her chest muscles were tight. Sweat drizzled down her neck, pooling in the hollow of her throat. Her knees wobbled. She'd never been so terrified.

The beefy palm lifted. Her lips felt crushed, bruised.

"What do you want from me?" she whispered.

"No talking, remember?" The man trailed the gun from her temple down her cheek, then clamped a hand on her shoulder. "My, you are a pretty one. I like your yellow hair. I can see why that detective keeps sniffing 'round here. Too bad he ain't here to save you now, though." The creep emitted a harsh bark of sadistic laughter.

She could smell the strong stench of alcohol on him, and her stomach churned.

"I'd enjoy putting a bullet through him."

Savannah stiffened. Had Ginger called the ambulance yet? Was it on its way? What about Matt? Had she called him, too?

"Yes, indeed, you are one fine little filly." The corrupt hand at her waist inched up under her shirt. Rough fingers grabbed at her breast, squeezing hard. The joke was on him. She didn't have any sensation in her augmented breasts since the mastectomy and reconstruction surgery.

He mashed his mouth to her ear and ground his hips

against her back in a lewd gesture. "What say me and you have some fun?"

Savannah stayed rigid, silently infuriated but unable to act on her rage. She had to remain calm, retain her wits.

"Oh, you're one of them cold-blooded types, huh? Too good for the likes of me." He leaned closer, jamming the gun into her tender flesh. "Well, I'm gonna make you be nice to me, one way or the other."

Savannah gulped and willed herself not to faint.

16

Matt did not pull into the driveway of the Circle B. Instead, he parked a few yards down the road, unholstered his duty weapon, and crept through the pasture, dodging behind mesquite trees and sagebrush in an attempt to stay out of sight.

He sought out Joe's hiding place behind the barn and discovered the abandoned patrol car. Swearing under his breath, Matt scanned the area and spotted Joe on his back beneath a tree.

"Joe." He sprinted over and squatted next to the downed man. Joe groaned, and his eyes fluttered open. "You okay?"

"Matt? That you? I can't see so good. My vision is blurry."

Matt helped Joe to a sitting position. "What happened?"

"They ambushed me." Joe grimaced, raising a hand to the back of his head. "I heard a noise, went to investigate, and they got me from behind."

Matt fingered the large goose egg blossoming on the back of Joe's head.

"Can you stand up?"

"I can try." Joe struggled to dig his feet into the sandy soil, but when he tried to stand, his knees buckled. He groaned. "I feel dizzy."

"Okay." Matt stroked his jaw with a thumb and forefinger. "Forget standing. If I drag you over to the car, do you think you can call for backup?"

"Yeah. I can handle that."

Grunting with the effort, Matt laced his arms under Joe's upper torso and tugged him over to the patrol cruiser. "It's up to you to get me some help, buddy. I'm going after Larkins and Thompson."

"Right."

Leaving Joe behind, Matt turned toward the Circle B. He was so damned stupid. How could he have ever left Savannah and the baby alone, even with Joe on watch, certain that Thompson and Larkins would come back to the ranch? He'd underestimated those two, and his lapse in judgment could cost Savannah her life.

No. Not as long as breath inhabited his body.

He moved faster, crouching low until he arrived parallel with the driveway. He caught a glimpse of Savannah's compact car, saw the passenger door hanging open. The sight alarmed him even more.

He wanted to burst forth, guns blazing, Savannah's name on his lips, but he had to be smart, size up the situation. Evaluate the circumstances. Quickly, he glanced at the house and saw a face pressed against the window. Savannah?

His fear dissipated a bit. Had he overreacted?

Uncertain of what awaited him, Matt proceeded with caution, slowly circling the house. He saw Clem's pickup sitting at the west pasture gate, but no sign of the ranch hand. From his vantage point, he could see the back of the barn and part of the farmyard.

He hunkered behind an outcropping of rocks, watching, waiting.

No movement. No noise. No anything. He didn't like this one bit. The whole atmosphere was suspicious.

He ran a hand along his jaw, anxiety corkscrewing through his stomach. He still loved her with an intensity that frightened him. For two years, he'd tried to convince himself he'd gotten over her, but the bare truth was that he would never get over her. They might not ever solve their problems and build a life together, but he would never be free of his desire for her. She was as much a part of him as his own flesh and bone.

And he would die for her if necessary.

Shifting his weight, he consulted his watch. Only ten minutes had passed since he'd first walked onto the ranch. Ten minutes of prolonged agony. Should he go to the house or stay put?

He muttered a curse. Every tissue in his body cried for combat, to vanquish an enemy, but such rash action might prove fatal.

Still undecided, he crept closer. His gaze swept the area. A breeze rustled the trees. He looked down and saw a chewed red cocktail straw lying in the sand. Fear torqued him. The muscles in his hand strained as he clasped his gun tighter. If they'd harmed one strand of Savannah's lovely honey hair, Matt would hunt them to the ends of the earth.

He had to act, but what was the right thing to do?

Rising to a standing position, he skirted a clump of cacti, sidled up to the barn, and pressed his body against the corrugated tin. With his gun drawn, he inched along the side until he came to the corner. Taking a deep breath to fortify himself, he sprang around the barn, his 9mm firearm clutched in both hands.

That's when he saw Clem's body.

BRENT LARKINS'S DIRTY FINGERS CLAWED AT HER BLOUSE.

Frantically, Savannah tried to think. She wanted to scream, but her tongue seemed welded to the roof of her mouth. Where was Hootie Thompson? Had he cornered Ginger and Cody in the house? Was that why neither the ambulance nor Matt had shown up yet?

Not knowing if she could count on being rescued, she had to save herself.

"Oh, you're a hot one," Larkins groaned, rubbing his slimy hand along her skin.

Savannah shuddered, repulsed. Her gaze raked the area, desperately seeking a weapon, racking her brain for some hint of a plan.

And then she saw it.

The muzzle of Gary's shotgun pointing out from its place behind the door. She caught her breath, afraid to hope. Could she get away from Larkins and make it across the barn to the weapon?

Clearing her throat, Savannah wet her lips. "I could get into this a little more if you weren't holding a gun to my head."

"Ah, no, babe. I ain't that stupid. Besides, I like having sex with a gun in my hand. It's a real kick." He traced the cold, hard nose of his gun against her chin.

She bit her tongue to choke back the bile rising in her throat, but she couldn't risk making him angry. He reeked of whiskey, and she didn't know what this low-life snake was capable of.

"Where...where's your friend?" she asked hoarsely.

His raucous laugh grated her nerves. "I suppose he's in the house, making the acquaintance of your little sister."

Savannah moaned as he voiced her worst fear. "Please," she begged. "Do what you want to me, but leave my son and my sister out of this."

Vicious images of what could be transpiring in the house raced through her mind like a raging forest fire. As an answer, Larkins turned her around to face him, one hand on her shoulder, the other loosely gripping his gun.

"I'm gonna do what I want, either way," he said, then dipped his head and sucked on her neck.

Savannah took advantage of the only opportunity she might have. With one swift movement, she plowed her knee into his groin. Larkins's grunt of pain brought her a moment of brief satisfaction. He dropped to his knees, clutching at his wounded crotch.

Spinning away from him, Savannah ran for the barn door and Gary's gun.

The outlaw cursed her. She heard him cock the hammer of his revolver. She stopped. Her arm inches from the door, blood strumming madly through her veins.

"You're gonna pay for that," he growled, staggering to his feet.

Should she go for Gary's gun and risk getting shot?

Larkins lurched forward, his ugly face twisted into a mask of rage, his pistol pointed right at her head.

"Drop the gun, Larkins." Matt's voice cut through the roaring in her head. He'd come!

Her heart sang with joy. She turned to stare at him. Her hero.

Matt's full attention was trained on his quarry. His eyes were narrowed, harsh, demanding. His gun poked at Larkins's head. He looked as substantial as a rock—powerful, immovable. Savannah's heart swelled with love for him. No matter what else, Matt was one hell of a lawman.

"Damn you, Forrester!" Larkins shouted.

"Put the gun down, Larkins," Matt ordered, his voice hard, serious steel. "Don't make me kill you."

The timbre of Matt's voice quaked Savannah to her toes.

Her man was fierce, protective, a mountain range of strength and power. His job defined him—ambitious, fair, bold, loyal, brave—excellent qualities for either a lawman.

Or a husband.

Larkins kept his gun leveled at Savannah's heart. "You're bluffing, Forrester. You put *your* gun down, or the lady gets it."

❧

MATT HESITATED.

He stood behind Clem's prostrate body, feet wide apart, gun gripped in both hands like a lifeline. He wanted nothing more than to rid the world of Brent Larkins forever, but Savannah was in his line of fire. Could he get off a shot before Larkins did? Did he dare take the chance?

No. He couldn't risk it.

"Who's got the upper hand now, lawman?" Larkins taunted. "Looks like you didn't think this one through. That little wench got you rattled. Screwed up your thinking."

Matt clenched his teeth. Larkins was right. His concern for Savannah superseded common sense. He'd burst in, prepared to save her, only to find the tables turned for lack of proper planning. He'd made a grave error, worse than any rookie. He'd let his emotions rule him.

Savannah's eyes widened in fear. Those beautiful gold-green eyes should never have to experience the ugly side of life. She deserved to be shielded, protected. She'd trusted him, and he'd failed her. Just like he'd failed her that night in Kelly's when his ego had him rushing to Jackie Spencer's defense and getting shot in the process.

If he lived to be a hundred, he'd never forget the expression reflected on Savannah's face. She'd lost her faith in his ability to save her. Anybody could see that. What kind of lawman was he, that he couldn't safeguard the one person he loved most in the whole world?

This was why she hadn't confided in him about the breast cancer gene, and later why she hadn't tried harder to tell him that she was pregnant with Cody. She'd lost her faith in him.

"Throw down your gun, Forrester," Larkins repeated.

"Where's Thompson?" Matt asked, stalling for time. His mind raced, quickly reviewing and discarding his options. How to solve this dilemma?

"Right here, Detective."

Matt whirled to see Hootie Thompson approaching from the house, a rifle in his hand. "You'd better do as Brent asked and put your gun away."

Faced with the inevitable, Matt tossed his firearm to the dirt and raised his hands above his head.

"Yahoo! Ain't that a pretty sight, Brent? A defeated lawman without a gun and completely at our mercy," Thompson gloated.

"You got them cows loaded in the trailer?" Larkins asked, stepping across the barn to grasp Savannah by the elbow. She tried to shake him off, but he clung to her like a grass burr.

The sight rankled Matt. He clenched his jaw. He wanted to wrap his bare hands around Brent Larkins's disgusting throat and squeeze until the man turned purple.

"Yep," Thompson answered Larkins. "Got six Gerts loaded and made a good haul in the house, too. Three hundred dollars and a pair of diamond earrings."

"What did you do to my son and my sister?" Savannah shouted.

Matt glanced at her. All fear had fled from her lovely face. If anything, she looked indignant.

Hootie Thompson strolled over, leaned down, picked up Matt's gun, and stuck it in the waistband of his pants. "I didn't do nothin' to your precious family. Your little sister is tied up, and the kid's asleep," Thompson drawled.

"You ought to be more concerned about yourself," Brent Larkins said, leering at Savannah and gesturing toward her with his pistol. Matt fought to keep from lunging the distance and attacking Larkins. He couldn't save anyone if he got shot. "Looks like we're gonna have to take a hostage, and I prefer you to the lawman. You smell better."

Hostage?

The word sent a stab of fear knifing through Matt's body. He would not allow them to take Savannah away from the Circle B. He would die first.

"Yeah." Hootie giggled. "She'd make real sweet company."

"Come here," Larkins said to Thompson. "You take the girl while I deal with the lawman."

"Don't hurt him," Savannah pleaded. Her eyes met Matt's, desperate, scared, but struggling hard to be brave.

Impotent rage coursed through his blood. He wanted to make them pay for what they were doing to her. Larkins and Thompson would never get away with this. If only he could disarm them. But how? Matt cast a glance around, trying desperately to devise a plan.

"Keep your hands up," Hootie snarled. He walked past Matt on his way to join Larkins in the barn, his rifle pointed at Matt's midsection.

From the corner of his eye, Matt saw Clem move ever so slightly. A flicker of hope leaped in him. Was the old man conscious? Had he been listening? On the off chance Clem might actually be able to help, Matt moved, lowering his arms to divert Hootie's attention.

"Hey!" Larkins hollered, one arm around Savannah's neck. "Hootie, watch your prisoner. Don't let him put his arms down. Search him for another gun."

Hootie stalked forward, eyes on Matt. He never looked

down. Clem reached out a hand, tripping Hootie as he walked past.

Hootie fell flat on his face, and the rifle flew from his arms.

Matt plunged on top of the downed man, crushing him under his weight.

Savannah screamed.

Larkins cursed.

Chaos ensued.

17

The minute Clement Olson tripped Thompson, Savannah, alert for any opportunity to turn the tables and escape, sank her teeth into Larkins's forearm.

The man cried out and lost his grip on the handgun. It clattered to the ground. Savannah kicked the revolver across the floor.

"Run, Savannah, run," Matt shouted from outside the barn door where he grappled with Hootie Thompson.

She refused to abandon her man. Determined to protect Matt to the death if necessary, she lunged for Gary's shotgun behind the barn door.

Abruptly, her head snapped back, and pain shot down her neck as Larkins grabbed her ponytail and jerked. But Savannah would not be stopped. Like a bobcat, she turned on him, arms and legs flailing. She scratched, kicked, spat.

Larkins stared, shocked.

Twisting free from his grip, she lowered her head and butted him in the stomach. The big man grunted and sank to his knees.

Savannah sprang for the shotgun once more, and this time came up victorious. She aimed the muzzle at the ceiling, then pulled the trigger. The resounding boom captured everyone's attention. Bits of roof rained down around them.

"Nobody move," she shouted.

All four men stared at her. She was the only one standing, the only one with a weapon.

"You." She glared at Larkins and swung the shotgun around to point it at him. "Face down on the floor. Arms on the back of your head. I'm sure you know the position."

Larkins sneered but obeyed her.

Clem moaned, rolled over, and tried to get to his feet.

"Stay put, Clem," she said. "An ambulance is on the way."

"One should be here soon," Matt said, climbing off Thompson. "Joe called for backup." He dragged the outlaw to his feet, pulled handcuffs from his back pocket, and snapped them around his wrists as he read him his rights.

"What happened to Joe?"

"These bushwhackers got him, too," Matt said ruefully.

"Here comes the cavalry." The wail of sirens brought a smile to Savannah's face. Suddenly, she felt invincible. Not only had she survived the ordeal, but she had also triumphed. Was this the heady feeling that possessed Matt each time he made an arrest? Perhaps she could understand his penchant for law enforcement, after all. "Late as always."

Matt grinned. "Guess you fellas tangled with the wrong woman, eh?"

While Matt handcuffed Larkins and read him his rights, Savannah said, "I'm going to check on Ginger and Cody."

Tossing her head, she marched past the men and into the farmhouse. She found Ginger tied to a chair in the kitchen, a gag in her mouth.

The sight tore a hole clean through her heart. This was the flip side of law enforcement. The side that hurt. Innocent victims caught in the middle. Savannah swallowed hard as she realized for the first time what Matt went through to do his job well. Clenching her jaw, Savannah took a knife from the drawer and sawed through the ropes binding her little sister.

Ginger pulled the gag from her mouth. "Oh, Vannah!" She embraced her sister. "I was so scared. I came inside to call 911, but then that awful man jumped out of the closet and ambushed me."

"Did he hurt you?" Savannah's stomach constricted.

Ginger shook her head. "He just said rude things and stole your secret money."

"I'm so sorry, Gin," she whispered, hugging her sister tightly. "So very sorry."

"It's okay." Ginger patted her arm.

"Come on." Savannah took her sister by the hand. "Let's go get Cody."

The sight of her son sleeping in his crib, his little face stained with salty tear tracks, almost undid her. How could she have been so foolish as to place this tiny child in jeopardy? She should have heeded Matt's warning and checked into a hotel. What kind of mother was she?

Ginger placed a hand on Savannah's shoulder. "It's all right, sis. Cody's fine. I'm fine. We survived."

Savannah tugged Cody from his bed and held him close. What would have happened to him if she'd been hurt or killed out there in the barn? Tears burned her eyes as her whole body trembled. Unable to trust her legs to support her, Savannah sank down into the rocking chair and breathed a prayer of gratitude that all had survived.

MATT SQUATTED BESIDE CLEM, WAITING FOR BACKUP FROM the sheriff's office and the ambulance to appear. He held the shotgun across his lap and never took his eyes off Larkins and Thompson, who lay prostrate on the ground in front of him, their hands cuffed behind their backs.

More than anything, he wanted to be with Savannah, cradling her in his arms, soothing her. She needed his comfort right now, but he was stuck here.

For once, the arrest had not been satisfying. Usually, he felt an uplifting kick, a mental high from bringing outlaws to justice. But this time he felt empty, unhappy. There was no sense of accomplishment in knowing he'd been responsible for orchestrating this disaster. He'd never meant to involve Savannah or cause her harm. He'd only been doing his duty.

His job.

Lawman.

The role that defined him. The job he thought he loved more than anything. But a job couldn't keep him warm at night or fuss over him when he was sick or exhausted. A job was simply a way to make money—it shouldn't be an identity or an excuse for a life.

He felt vacuous, hollow.

The nearing wail of sirens drew his attention. He got to his feet. "Well, fellas looks like your escort has arrived."

Larkins cursed him.

"Anybody ever tell you that you're a sore loser, Brent?" Matt drawled, but he took no pleasure in goading the thief. Somewhere, somehow, the whole process had lost its magic.

Two sheriff's deputies hustled into the barn to transport Larkins and Thompson to the county jail just about the same time the paramedics showed up to whisk Clem and Joe off to the hospital in Rascal.

Fifteen minutes later, Matt stood alone in the yard. Neither Savannah nor Ginger had come outside. Matt took a deep breath. He had to see Savannah before returning to the sheriff's department to write up the paperwork. He had to tell her how sorry he was. Had to make sure she was okay.

Bolstering his courage, he knocked on the back door.

Ginger peered out. Her gold-green eyes, so like Savannah's, stared at him. "Hey, Matt."

"May I come inside?" he asked, hesitantly fingering his Stetson.

Ginger stood to one side as Matt passed through the doorway.

"Are you all right? Did Thompson hurt you?" Matt reached out to touch her shoulder.

Ginger shrugged as if she were cool, but she still looked shook up. "I'm fine. He just tied me up."

"I'm so sorry."

"Not your fault."

But it was. He should never have left Savannah alone. Should have never started this ploy to entice the thieves to come after her cattle again.

"Where's Todd?" Matt asked, remembering Ginger was supposed to be in Cancun on her honeymoon.

"We split up."

"What?" Matt looked at her, startled.

"Yeah."

"I hate to hear that." What a shame. Didn't anyone's relationship work out anymore? He saw tears glisten in Ginger's eyes, so he didn't press for details. "Maybe you guys can still work things out."

"Maybe," Ginger mumbled.

"Where's your sister?"

"She's in Cody's room."

Matt eased down the hallway. He felt like a grammar school kid going before the principal. Cody's bedroom door hung open a few inches. Matt peeked around the corner and saw Savannah rocking his son.

Their son.

Cody. The unbreakable bond between them.

"Hi." He stepped into the room.

She glanced up. "How are you doing?"

His eyes met hers. "That's what I was about to ask you."

"I'm okay." She nodded at Cody. "We're okay."

He cleared his throat. There was so much he wanted to say to her, he didn't know where to begin. "Uh... I'll need for you and Ginger to come down to the sheriff's office and give us an official statement."

She said nothing.

"Whenever you can. No hurry." He raised his palms. "I'm sure you need time to collect yourself."

"All right."

"Listen..."

"Yes?" She met his eyes again.

"We need to have a long talk, you and I."

"Not now, Matt. I have too much to sort through."

"Okay," he said because he didn't know what else to say. "I'll just head out then." He paused, waiting. Hoping she'd say something else. Tell him she loved him. Tell him she wanted them to be a forever family.

She did not.

"Savannah?"

"What is it?"

"I love you."

Her head shot up, and she speared him with her eyes. He yearned to hear her say it in return, and he clenched his fists, feeling the raw emotion claw at his insides.

"Goodbye, Matt."

"Goodbye then." He left the room, left her house, and he couldn't help feeling he was leaving everything important in the world behind him. He'd told her he loved her. She had not said it in return.

He'd been holding on to a pipe dream.

Two hours later, Ginger set a bowl of her homemade chicken noodle soup in front of Savannah. "I spoke with a nurse at the hospital, and she said Clem was in stable condition, but he's got a concussion. They treated Joe and released him."

"We'll have to go see Clem tomorrow." Savannah shoved the soup away. Her stomach was still roiling.

"Come on, sis. You've got to eat something." Ginger gently pushed the bowl toward her.

"Okay. I'll try." She picked up a spoon and stared into the bowl at the chicken, celery, carrots, and onions swimming in the hot broth. She put the spoon back down.

Try as she might, she could not shake the image of Matt's wounded face from her mind when he'd told her he loved her, and she had not said it in return. She'd cut him to the quick.

But she couldn't say the words she longed to say. She loved him. She had always loved him, and she wanted him to be in Cody's life. But what did she have to offer Matt? She was scarred from her surgeries. She was no longer the whole, young girl he'd known two years ago. She couldn't bear him any more children, and her whole life would be filled with worries about a cancer diagnosis. She couldn't saddle him with that burden.

You're doing it again. Making a unilateral decision for Matt. He should get to choose for himself what burdens he wants to carry.

Ginger plopped down in the kitchen chair next to her. Savannah angled a sidelong glance at her sister. "What about you and Todd? Did you ever get hold of him?"

Ginger nodded. "I called him in Cancun, and we talked. You were right. He was crazy with worry."

"I told you."

"I suppose I did behave like a spoiled brat."

"You got his attention, though."

"Boy, did I. He was so frantic, he had the local authorities combing the beach looking for my body." Ginger grinned. "I guess he really does care."

"Of course he cares. Anybody can see how much Todd loves you."

"Just the way Matt loves you."

Savannah waved a hand. "Things between Matt and me are a different story."

"How's that?"

"I don't want to talk about Matt right now," Savannah said resolutely.

"Todd's catching the next plane home," Ginger said, tactfully respecting Savannah's wishes. "We're planning on some heavy-duty communicating. He's really upset with me, and I have a lot to make up for."

"I'm glad you decided to try to work things out. I like Todd. He's a good man. What made you change your mind?"

"Being tied up and threatened has given me a whole new perspective on things. Made me realize what was really important and how much I really do love Todd. When you get right down to it, love is the only thing that matters, isn't it?"

"I don't know," Savannah admitted. "I used to believe that once."

She loved Matt more than she ever thought possible. Despite the two years they'd spent apart, Savannah still loved him with a need that frightened her. That was it in a nutshell. She'd lost so much in her short life, and she was terrified to act on love.

"If you love someone unconditionally, you have to accept them as they are," Ginger said. "Matt's a lawman, and you have some health issues, but that doesn't mean you can't figure out a way to be together. Not if you really love each other and you both fight for each other."

"When did you get so smart?" Savannah lifted the corner of her mouth in a half-smile.

"I wanted to change Todd, make him over to suit me. But I have to face the fact he's a hard worker, and he's willing to invest his efforts in achieving his goals. I'm going to have to learn to live with the fact he might not always have as much time to spend with me as I might like."

"Are you sure you can live with that?"

Ginger beamed. "I really don't have a choice."

"What do you mean?"

"Because, Savannah, I just can't live without him."

Just like I can't live without Matt.

❧

Sheriff Langley clamped a hand on Matt's shoulder. "Are you sure about this, son?"

Inhaling sharply, Matt nodded. "Yes. It's a decision I should have made two years ago, but of course, I'll work the next weeks while you train someone else."

"I hate to lose you, Matt. You're one fine lawman."

Matt shook his head. "Some things are simply more important. It's time I invested my efforts elsewhere."

"That woman has gotten under your skin, hasn't she?"

Matt nodded. "Today, when I saw Larkins holding that gun on Savannah, I lost my objectivity. I reacted instead of acted. I was no longer in control. Knowing that I'd placed her in danger...? Well, Sheriff, I can't live with that."

"I understand. If you change your mind, you always have a job here."

"I appreciate it."

They shook hands.

"So, what are you going to do with yourself?"

The corner of Matt's mouth crooked. "Thought I might try my hand at teaching. I have a minor in secondary education. See if I can't reach those at-risk kids before they're too far gone."

Sheriff Langley considered the idea. "Yeah, you might be good at that, too. The things we do for love, huh?"

"A family man has to take care of himself," Matt said, plunking his hat down on his head. "I have a son now that I want to live to see grow up. That is, of course, if Savannah will have me."

"I wish you luck, partner."

"Thanks," Matt said. "I have a feeling I'm going to need it."

He walked out of the sheriff's department and squinted against the late-afternoon sun, his thoughts tumultuous.

He was a lawman, trained to be tough, fearless, and emotionally in control, but when it came to affairs of the heart, he was like anyone else. Insecure. Nervous. Downright scared of losing the one he loved.

But this time, he had to take a gamble. Because Savannah was worth the risk.

Two years ago, when she'd broken up with him over his job, he'd made a big mistake letting wounded pride and hurt feelings get in the way. Yes, he'd learned since then why she'd really broken up with him, but he'd been too stubborn to even consider a job change in those days. He wasn't going to make that same mistake twice.

So much lost time. So much heartache. He'd been granted a golden opportunity. A second chance to make things right. He wasn't going to blow it this time. So he surrendered his job in hopes he could persuade Savannah to surrender her heart.

Giving up his identity as a lawman gave him an unexpected sense of freedom. He could be anything he chose. A whole world loomed before him—open, free, just waiting to be explored. There was so much more to life than law enforcement. He could be a teacher, a rancher, a husband, a dad.

Those tender thoughts tugged at him, created a vortex of longing so great, he felt completely overwhelmed. He knew only one thing. He had to go to the Circle B, find Savannah, and say all the things he neglected to say two years ago.

He had to convince her to become his wife.

No matter what it took.

18

Savannah wheeled her compact car down the gravel road, heading for Rascal and the sheriff's department to give her statement concerning the events that had happened at the Circle B earlier that day. Ginger had stayed behind to watch Cody. Later, Ginger would go give her account of the incident, and then head out to pick Todd up at the San Antonio airport.

Ginger's words kept echoing through Savannah's brain like a refrain from a catchy tune. *If you love someone unconditionally, you have to accept them as they are.*

How true. Too bad it had taken two years, a heap of heartbreak, and a confrontation with outlaws to drive home that fact.

She loved Matt. Had loved him since she was twenty-one years old. But she'd been afraid to trust him to be there for her. When she discovered she carried the breast cancer gene, she'd been so afraid of his rejection that she'd rejected him first.

At least that way, she'd been in control, not a victim of fate. But by cutting him off and not even giving him a chance to stay by her side, she'd forfeited so much happiness, so much joy.

He'd told her he loved her. It was up to her to trust him and take him at his word.

Joy engulfed her as she realized lasting happiness might actually be within her grasp. She pushed down on the accelerator, spurring the little car faster. She had to find Matt, tell him just how much she loved him, too.

Matt saw Savannah's car whiz by him in a blur of blue. Immediately, he braked and did an erratic U-turn. She had to be doing at least seventy. Where was she headed in such an all-fired hurry?

She left him in a billow of dust.

Matt rolled down his window, then grinning, reached out to slap the portable siren onto the roof, gunned the Jeep, and took off after her. The siren wailing, he honked the horn and flashed his lights.

At last, she noticed him and pulled over onto the shoulder.

Matt glided to a stop behind her and threw the Jeep into Park. Without even shutting off the engine, he jumped out.

Her car door slammed closed at the same time his did.

She stood there, wearing a white sundress, the late-evening sun slanting through the soft material so he could see the shape of her slender legs right through the thin cotton. Her honey-blond hair framed her face in soft layers. The sight of her erected a wall of desire in his chest so strong and intense, he almost bit his tongue.

This was the woman he loved with all his heart and soul.

SAVANNAH SWALLOWED HARD, STARING AT THE TALL, DARK, and handsome man in front of her. For once he was hatless, his black hair ruffling in the wind from passing cars. His brown eyes glistened with a determined light. His hard, firm, tanned biceps just begging to be touched and caressed, bulged beneath the sleeves of his red cotton shirt.

Her arms trembled. Her mouth went dry. Her palms instantly were drenched with perspiration.

"Savvy," he said.

The sound came to her—deep, masculine, provocative. It stirred in her a crescendo of primal emotions. The voice of her lover. The voice lost to her so long ago through sadness and misunderstanding. The voice she'd dreamed of for two long, interminable years.

"Come here," he croaked and held his arms wide.

Savannah didn't remember crossing the few yards toward him. She only knew that suddenly she was melting into his embrace like parched ranchland soaking up water.

He planted his mouth on hers in a kiss so powerful, she could scarcely breathe.

Who needed air when she possessed Matt's lips as her lifeline, she wondered, inhaling the essence of him. Such heaven. Such bliss.

The world around her blurred. The cars flying by, the tinny sound of Matt's radio wafting through the open Jeep window, and the high grass tickling her shins. None of it penetrated her mind. She experienced only his welcoming kiss.

With thirsty need, he blanketed kisses on her eyelids, her nose, her cheeks, returning time and again to drink from her lips. She marveled at his desperate hunger, astonished she created such urgency in him.

His hands rubbed her neck. His fingers stroked her body, starting from her shoulder blades, kneading downward until both hands massaged the small of her back, then lower to cup her derriere.

He tugged his mouth from her jaw, then nestled his face at the intersection of her throat and shoulder. He nibbled lightly, sending waves of delight contracting throughout her body. She laced her fingers together behind his neck, clinging to this man as if her very life depended on him.

Savannah absorbed his neediness, felt his hands tremble with excitement. She thrilled to the flagrant evidence of his growing passion. A passion equaled only by her own starving fervor.

And the ground shifted beneath her as Matt lifted her off her feet and held her aloft, pressing her tight to his chest like an impossible treasure. A surreal sensation washed over her. She'd dreamed of this reunion for so long, it seemed too good to be true.

She kneaded her fingers through his thick thatch of hair. He kissed her long and hard. A serious kiss by a man who was in love. Joy exploded inside her. Was it true? Did he still love her as he once had? Did he love her as much as she loved him?

The sky was bluer than it had ever been, the sight of his dear face so achingly tender that she wanted to cry. His mouth tasted sweeter than any confection ever concocted. His touch was more evocative than any romantic movie ever filmed. His scent was fragrant than a thousand spices.

Then she heard it. Their song on the radio, radiating out into the gathering dusk, surrounding them, engulfing them, welding them as one. The song he'd played for her on his guitar the very first night they met. "The Twelfth of Never."

Tears came to her eyes and rolled down her cheeks.

"Savvy?" he asked with a quiver in his voice. Gently he set her down and looked into her eyes, concern knitting his brow.

"It's okay," she said, smiling at him through the blur of tears. She swiped at her eyes with the back of her hand. "I'm just so happy."

He gathered her close again. "You belong to me, Savannah Raylene. You know that, don't you? Even when you married Gary, we still belonged together. You do understand what I'm saying, don't you?"

"You don't mind that I can no longer have children?"

"We've got Cody."

"My body is—"

"Beautiful."

"I was on my way to find you. I wanted to tell you the same thing. Matt, I accept you unconditionally. You are a lawman, that's who you are, and I love you for it."

Matt looked surprised, then a chuckle rumbled through him.

"What's so funny?"

"I'm not a lawman anymore. I quit my job today."

"Matt!"

"Yep."

"You did that for me?"

"Two years ago, I chose my career over you. I was wrong, Savannah. You are the most important thing in the world to me. No job, no career, no vocation should come between us."

"But you love your job," she protested.

"I'll find another job to love."

"What will you do?" she fretted.

"Who knows? I might go to law school. I've also thought about teaching high school. Hell,

I might even put Pat Langley's nose out of joint and run for sheriff."

Savannah shook her head. "You can't quit because of me. Eventually, you'd resent it. You're not the desk-job type."

"It's my choice."

"I love you for you, and you're a lawman."

"Savvy, you and Cody are more important than all the jobs in the world."

"You've got to call Sheriff Langley and get your job back," she insisted.

He threaded his fingers through his hair. "I feel like a character in an O. Henry story."

"After that standoff in the barn today with Larkins and Thompson, I finally realized how much your work means to you. You're a superb detective. It would be a shame for you to quit. And if I love you, I accept you as you are. Just as you accept me, scars, breast cancer gene, and all."

"Don't you get it, honey? I no longer want to be at the wrong end of some outlaw's gun. I want you and Cody. Taking such risks is for bachelors."

"Matt," she whispered. "What are you saying?"

"Marry me, Savannah. We can work everything else out. Let's make a real family for Cody."

"Oh, Matt." She sighed.

"Well?" He cocked one eyebrow. "What do you say?"

"I say yes, my darling, oh, yes."

Gazing into Matt's eyes, Savannah saw his love shining back at her, as deep and real as her own feelings for him. Her chest tightened. An overflow of happiness inflated her heart. The loneliness and misery of the last two years were instantly swept away.

Fresh tears choked her throat. Rapture bubbled inside her. She'd learned to trust him and with that trust came a serenity she'd never before experienced. From now on, nothing would ever separate them.

"I've grown a lot, too," he said, holding both her hands in his. "I've learned false pride is a dangerous thing. I almost lost you because I was too damned stubborn to admit I was hurt."

"We sure put each other through the wringer, didn't we?" She smiled.

"Ah, but, Savvy, there's only one good thing about breaking up."

"And that is?"

"The kissing and making up."

"Since our fight lasted two years, I can't wait to see what the reconciliation is going to be like."

He bent his head and feathered another kiss along her lips. "I love you, Savannah Raylene Prentiss Markum."

"I love you, too, Matthew Cody Forrester. Now let's go home," she replied, her voice coming out husky. "I can't wait to get to the making up part."

"Me, either, babe. Me, either."

EPILOGUE

"Congratulations, Sheriff Forrester." Todd Baxter grinned at his brother-in-law. "How does it feel to be the youngest man ever elected sheriff in this county?"

"I can't tell a lie," Matt said. "It feels fantastic. My only regret is that a heart attack forced Pat Langley to retire. Of course, if it weren't for Savannah here, I would still be on the front lines getting shot at."

Matt reached across the dinner table and patted his wife's hand. She smiled back, and that familiar arrow of joy shot clean through him. Marrying Savvy had been the best move he'd ever made. It was two days after the election, and they were sitting at the kitchen table having a small family celebration.

"But don't you miss the excitement, the sense of adventure that comes with being in the field?" Todd asked. "Even just a little bit?"

"Daddy," Cody insisted loudly. "Piggyback ride." The boy grabbed Matt's fingers and tugged.

"Are you kidding?" Matt responded to Todd. "Tracking

hard-core felons would be a sedate change of pace from raising a three-and-a-half-year-old." Matt cast a sideways glance at Ginger's extended tummy. "But then, you'll find out soon enough."

"Now," Cody insisted.

"Come here, son." Matt hefted the boy into his lap. "Of course, three-week-olds aren't much tamer." Matt smiled at his brand-new baby daughter, Marissa Angelique, who they'd just adopted, as she lay sleeping in the bassinet parked next to the table. "Are they, Savvy?"

"And you were the one who always thrived on danger," Savannah said. "I think that's a far-fetched story. One dirty diaper and you're done for."

Matt never could have imagined it, but the thrills and trials of being a father were unequaled. And his love for Savannah had never burned as brightly as it had the day they'd said: "I do." At that moment, he'd known his life was totally complete.

SAVANNAH SMILED AT HER HUSBAND. OVER THE PAST YEAR, their love had grown, expanding into a bright, shining thing so wonderful she scarcely believed her own happiness. But this time, she wasn't afraid of losing him.

Her life had swelled to overflowing. She was proud of Matt and his new career. He'd spent the last two years helping her get the ranch operating in the black, and now he'd won the sheriff's seat by a landslide.

And looking after Cody and Marissa left no room in her mind for worry. For the first time since her mother's death, Savannah felt unencumbered by fear. Matt's love had given her the key to freedom. He would be there to share her concerns, in good times and in bad.

The back door swung open, and Clem stepped in. "Miss Savannah," he said. "Looks like we got trouble."

"What is it, Clem?" Matt asked, setting Cody on the floor and pushing back from the table. Alarmed, Savannah stood up beside him.

"Two of them Gerts are trying to deliver at the same time. I'm gonna need some help out here. We had no idea what we were getting into when we got them all back."

Savannah breathed in a sigh of relief. Living on a ranch was never dull, and neither was life with Matt.

"Well, Savvy, are you sorry you married me?" Matt asked, a wry grin on his face. He retrieved his Stetson from the hat rack and settled it onto his head.

"Never," she whispered.

"You love me?" he asked, stepping over to give her a quick kiss.

"With all my soul."

"For how long?" he asked, one eyebrow cocked as they exchanged their daily repartee.

"Until the twelfth of never," she replied, her heart singing with joy. "I'll still be loving you."

DEAR READER, I HOPE YOU HAVE ENJOYED READING, *MATT*.

If you have the time, I would so appreciate a review. Just a couple of words will do. Thank you so much for leaving a review. You are appreciated!

Thank you for reading.

—Much love, Lori Wilde

If you would like to read more Texas Rascals, the third book in the series is *Nick*. Visit Lori on the Web @ www.lori-wilde.com

Sign up for news of Lori's latest releases on her website.

ABOUT LORI WILDE

Lori Wilde is the New York Times, USA Today and Publishers' Weekly bestselling author of 85 works of romantic fiction. She's a three time Romance Writers' of America RITA finalist and has four times been nominated for Romantic Times Readers' Choice Award. She has won numerous other awards as well.

Her books have been translated into 26 languages, with more than four million copies of her books sold worldwide.

Her breakout novel, The First Love Cookie Club, has been optioned for a TV movie.

ALSO BY LORI WILDE

In the *Texas Rascals Series*

Book 1 Keegan

Book 3 Nick

Book 4 Kurt

Book 5 Kael

Book 6 Brodie

Book 7 Truman

Book 8 Tucker

Book 9 Dan

PRAISE FOR LORI WILDE

“Wilde presents compelling evidence that love can make a person see stars and hear wedding bells with a single kiss.”

—Kirkus

*****Starred review ***** Readers will cheer for the wounded warrior who may just have found a place to call home.--*Publisher's Weekly*.

“Wilde’s writing is smooth and the story flows so well that it proves why she is one of the best in her genre. This book is a fabulous addition to her already stellar library!”

—RT Magazine

*****Starred review*****

In the latest stellar addition to her Twilight, Texas, series, Wilde explores the subject of PTSD with great empathy and insight. Put this together with the author’s usual superbly nuanced characters, layers of emotion, and exquisite sexual tension, and you have a heart-wrenching and heartwarming tale that beautifully encapsulates all the love, hope, faith, and forgiveness of the holiday season.---Booklist

"A beautiful, feel good romance that will leave you with a smile...a wonderful tale to curl up with on a cold winter night."

—Romance Reviews Today

"In this holiday pleaser, Lori Wilde has cooked up another warm and wonderful romance. Readers are going to love it... truly is a gift that keeps giving."

—FreshFiction

Ms. Wilde does an amazing job of drawing her readers into the story."

—Joyfully Reviewed

Made in the USA
Middletown, DE
19 September 2019